I0587565

CRASHED

GOLD HOCKEY #12

ELISE FABER

CRASHED
BY ELISE FABER
Newsletter sign-up

This is a work of fiction. Names, places, characters, and events are fictitious in every regard. Any similarities to actual events and persons, living or dead, are purely coincidental. Any trademarks, service marks, product names, or named features are assumed to be the property of their respective owners, and are used only for reference. There is no implied endorsement if any of these terms are used. Except for review purposes, the reproduction of this book in whole or part, electronically or mechanically, constitutes a copyright violation.

CRASHED
Copyright © 2021 Elise Faber
Print ISBN-13: 978-1-63749-023-5
Ebook ISBN-13: 978-1-63749-022-8
Cover Art by Jena Brignola

GOLD HOCKEY SERIES

GOLD CAST OF CHARACTERS

Heroes and Heroines:

Brit Plantain (Blocked) — first female goalie in the NHL, loves boy bands

Stefan Barie (Blocked) — captain of the Gold

Sara Jetty (Backhand) — artist and figure skater

Mike Stewart (Backhand) —defenseman for the Gold, romance guru

Blane Hart (Boarding) — center for the Gold, number 22

Mandy Shallows (Boarding) — trainer and physical therapist

Max Montgomery (Benched) — defensemen for the Gold, giant nerd

Angelica Shallows (Benched) — engineer at RoboTech, also a giant nerd

Blue Anderson (Breakaway) — top forward in the league and for the Gold

Anna Hayes (Breakaway) — Max's former nanny, no relation to Kevin Hayes

Rebecca Stravokraus (Breakout) — Gold publicist, makes killer brownies, known at PR-Rebecca

Kevin Hayes (Breakout) — forward for the Gold, no relation to Anna Hayes

Rebecca Hallbright (Checked) — nutritionist for the Gold, plethora of delicious vegan recipes, known as Nutrionist-Rebecca

Gabe Carter (Checked) — doctor, head trainer for the Gold

Calle Stevens (Coasting) — assistant coach for the Gold, former national team member

Coop Armstrong (Coasting) — talented forward on the Gold, addicted to historical romance audiobooks

Mia Caldwell (Centered) — 5th degree black belt, brings the snark

Liam Williamson (Centered) — Gold forward finding his love for the game, charming and pushy in equal measures

Charlotte Harris (Charging) — new Gold GM, hates losing and the game Chubby Bunny

Logan Walker (Charging) — defensemen for the Gold, skills include: cockiness and being able to buy presents that make Charlotte squirm

Dani Eastbrook (Caged) — video coach for the Gold, tech nerd, could fix your computer in a flash, shy

Ethan Korhonen (Caged) — forward for the Gold, killer power play skills, known as Big Juicy Brain

Fanny Douglas (Crashed) — silver medalist, skating coach for the Gold

Brandon Cunningham (Crashed) — brown curls, penchant for hallways, Kaydon Lewis's agent

Devon Scott (Block & Tackle) — former player, current owner Prestige Media group

Becca Scott (Block & Tackle) — Devon's assistant

Additional Characters:

Bernard — head coach

Richie — equipment manager

Dan Plantain — Brit's brother

Diane Barie — Stefan's mom

Pierre Barie — Stefan's dad, owner of the Gold

Spence — former goalie, married to Monique, daughter Mirabel

Monique — married to Spence, former model

Mirabel — daughter of Spence and Monique

Mitch — Sara's boss

Allison and Sean — Blane's parents

Pascal — Devon Scott's security lead

Roger Shallows — Mandy's dad

Grant and Megan — Devon's parents

ONE

FANNY

Wine. Solitude.

The perfect duo.

Stephanie "Fanny" Douglas was well-used to both.

She'd been single for roughly . . . well, for roughly an eternity. (*Eternity,* in this case meaning, a decade). Which meant that she'd moved beyond lonely, beyond being concerned with how much wine she consumed in the evenings during the week—a bottle every other night—and on to enjoying the simple pleasures where she could.

Alone.

Just as she preferred.

Her cell buzzed, and she glanced down at the text from her friend, Dani, gasping when she saw the picture of the gleaming diamond ring on her finger. Then smiling. Because she'd helped Dani's boyfriend—fiancé now, she supposed—pick out the exquisite piece of jewelry.

Sparkling. Huge. *Perfect.*

Exactly as Dani warranted.

Because Dani was one of the good ones, and she deserved the

good that Ethan brought into her life. Luckily, Ethan recognized the gift he'd been given when her shy, lovely friend had opened herself up to his love, and he treated her with care.

So, Fanny didn't have to kill him.

Off the ice, that was.

Off it, killing the built, six-foot-several inches, two-hundred-and-something-pound forward would be difficult for her five-foot-three, one-hundred-and-thirty-pound self. She was softer than her figure skating competition days—though she was still tough with a competitive streak that had never faded—but even more muscle wouldn't give her the ability to take down the professional hockey player.

But that was okay. Because if he hurt her friend, she could always kill him *on* the ice.

Fanny was the skating coach for the Gold—having made the jump from the Gold's AHL affiliate (minor league team) a few seasons before—and being part of a team that wasn't new, and had won the Cup twice now in their short tenure, meant they had the resources to hire people like her. She'd been running her own skating company before the Gold had brought her on to the payroll with the Rush, and while she still ran her business (clinics, private lessons for NHLers and other professional hockey players during the off-season, and other classes throughout the year for everyone from beginners to those hoping to make the big leagues), her main priority was picking apart the guys' skating skills and improving on everything from edge work to weight distribution.

She loved it.

The guys were awesome.

And being able to threaten them with extra skating drills meant that she was feared and revered in equal parts.

Exactly as she liked. *Muhaha.*

Her phone buzzed again—a collection of emojis that had Fanny grinning, and she typed out an enthusiastic response (with emojis a plenty), sent it, then set her cell on the counter, her smile fading, the joy she had for her friend dissipating like fog receding from over the Golden Gate. "Don't go there, Fanny," she murmured as she blinked rapidly, the memories pulling at the edges of her mind, threatening to claw her apart, to bring her back down into a place she'd barely survived the first time.

But it was hard *not* to go back there.

Years ago, she'd had what Dani now had. The fairy tale, the once upon a time. True love that had been tested and rebuilt stronger. A man who adored her. The diamond ring, the loving fiancé, the wonderful, effervescent hope for a future and a happily ever after.

But it *had* all been taken away. Seized for good, even though she'd fought so, *so* hard to keep hold of it.

Ripped from her as she'd tried on wedding dresses.

"Fate can be a real asshole sometimes," she muttered, moving to the counter and setting down her wineglass—her *big* wineglass. She was most definitely happy for her friend because she wasn't the kind of woman who wanted everyone else to be miserable just because her happy ending hadn't worked out.

Shit happened.

Unfortunately, a heap of that shit of life had landed on her shoulders. Twice.

She opened the fridge, pulled out the stopper on her bottle of wine, and poured a generous splash into her glass.

And then—remembering the lovely diamond ring that had once sat on her own finger—she poured another long splash.

"Come on, Fan," she murmured, knowing she was talking to herself, having an entire conversation with herself, in fact, and that wasn't good. But also knowing that it was a desperate bid to snap her out of her memories, so she was going with it. "You're going to change into pajamas," she continued, "put on a face mask, and watch the *Saw* franchise until you forget all about failed romances and remember that you have a very fulfilling life."

She paused, considered that.

Then nodded once, proud of her very sound plan.

Bringing her wine with her, since it was the first step of necessary oblivion (more wine first, gory horror flicks second), she made her way upstairs and into her bedroom, slipping into pajamas even though it was barely five in the evening.

Probably she should do something productive. Review tape of the guys, plan her next clinic, return emails from an inbox she never seemed to get ahead of nowadays.

But . . . she didn't want to.

"Plan, Douglas," she muttered. "Stick with the plan."

Right.

Wine. Check. Pajamas. Check. Face mask. Next on the agenda.

She washed her face, reached for the very expensive jar, smeared on the cream, and then she belted on her robe, grabbed her glass, and headed back downstairs, plugging a food order into her cell for the fattiest, greasiest carb load she could find.

In forty-five minutes, she was going to be at a great place.

Nearing a heart attack.

But all the happier for it.

"Movie," she whispered, cueing it up as she popped some popcorn—because if she was going for greasy and fatty, she needed that, too.

Pretty soon, she was on the couch, the slasher flick rolling, popcorn in her tummy, the buttery fingers of one hand gripping her wine, the other swiping fast and furious on TikTok while she giggled like a loon . . . and feeling so much better for it. There was no thought of unhappy endings, no heartbreak and pain.

Just actors on a screen playing a part. Just funny people making her laugh spouting about things she'd never even considered.

Plus, a nice buzz floating through her brain, softening the edges of the past, until she could almost pretend that she hadn't *ever* had a diamond ring, or a fiancé, or a twice-broken heart. Just random dates from men who never lasted long, whose sole purpose was to keep the matchmakers of the Gold—because hockey players were the *worst* gossips and busybodies—at bay.

She wouldn't think about the past, about Brandon—

The doorbell rang, just in the nick of time, chasing his name, the memories from her mind.

Thank God for *that*.

She paused the movie before jumping up and hurrying down the hall toward the front door, wine in one hand, still clutching her phone in the other, while doing her best to ignore the reminders of *him* that were chasing her like the hounds of hell. At least her food had arrived early. Stuffing her face would take her mind further off everything that had happened.

Fumbling with her cell, she flicked the lock, turned the handle, and pulled open the door, expecting to see a delivery person with a bag in hand.

Instead, she saw . . .

She blinked.

But . . . that was impossible.

The wine had gone to her head, because *he* could not be on her porch. She was hallucinating. That was it. Or drunk because the alcohol content of the pinot noir was higher than she'd expected. This was food, the delivery from—her eyes darted to her cell—Melissa, and that was all. A.L.L. *All.*

"Hey, baby."

His voice was—God, it brushed along her nape, drifted down her spine, caressed her abdomen, reached inside her rib cage, and dug its claws into her heart, slicing deep.

"Brandon?" she whispered, all her denials of *him* flitting away as the figment of her imagination stepped forward, the shadows disappearing from his face.

"It's me, Fan." He swiped a finger down her face and lifted it to his nose, inhaling deeply, the pale pink clay mixture staining his skin. "Still the same," he murmured, those claws digging deeper, goose bumps prickling to life on her arms, lifting the hairs there, causing her knees to tremble. "God, I missed this." A beat. "God, I missed *you.*"

Her lips parted, every cell inside her waiting for his next words, knowing they would change everything.

"I remember," he murmured. "I remember *everything.*"

Her buttery fingers spasmed, and she lost her hold on her wine.

The goblet fell to the porch. Glass shattered. Red splattered all over her bare feet. The shards glittered like malformed diamonds in the evening light.

"No," she whispered, her breath catching. "Oh, no. Not again."

The silence between them was terrible.

Almost as terrible as the clawed memories tearing into her, ripping everything open, making her *remember*—the diagnosis, the treatments, him being so sick, her at his side, the surgery, him looking at her blankly, not knowing her . . . and then the cancer coming back and going through that all over again.

Nausea twisted her stomach and she gagged, thinking for a moment the popcorn she'd consumed was going to make a reappearance.

She *couldn't.*

She couldn't go through that all again. She couldn't have this man be the most important thing in her life and then lose him.

Not when she'd been so thoroughly broken after the second time.

"Fanny," Brandon said, stepping toward her, cupping her jaw, and she gagged again. He'd touched her face, swiped off some of the mask, but she'd still been hoping he was some drunken apparition. She couldn't pretend, not when she felt his fingers, slightly roughened at the tips, stroking along her throat, gently encircling her wrist. "Look at me, baby," he said quietly. "Breathe. It's okay."

The soft command loosened the stranglehold on her abdomen, eased the queasiness.

She breathed.

She didn't lose the popcorn.

"There you go," he said, smoothing back her hair. "It's okay."

Fanny didn't think that would be the case, not in any way, shape, or form. But still, she found herself leaning into him and when that wasn't close enough, she started to step forward.

"No," he said, slightly sharp, nudging her back, and she realized she'd nearly trodden over the shards of glass.

Her throat worked, tried for words.

Failed to summon those words.

"I . . . um . . ."

Fanny blinked at the strange voice, saw the girl with the paper bag of food. Ah, *there* was Melissa.

"I have a delivery for Stephanie?"

"That's me," Fan managed, and Brandon stepped back, took the bag from the girl, and plunked it into Fanny's hands. "Thank you," he said, tone polite but dismissive.

"Are you okay?" Melissa asked, looking between the two of them, the broken glass on the porch. "Do you need me to . . ."

Fanny finally unfroze, mostly because Melissa was great.

She nodded at the girl, heart squeezing at the concern the other younger woman was displaying. Solidarity, and all that. "Thank you for asking," she said, releasing a slow breath. "But I'm really okay."

"You sure?"

Brandon stiffened as her eyes went from him to Fanny again. "I am."

Melissa nodded, disappearing back down the driveway. Fanny heard the soft *thunk* of a door closing, the faint rumble of an engine starting up. A moment later, it was quiet again.

"Can I come in?"

Her pieced-together heart pulsed—hope and old pain all twining together, but she didn't step back, didn't invite him in. Not yet. Not—

"You remember . . . me? Us?" she asked, staring up into his deep brown eyes, trying to discern the truth. Because the last time she'd seen him, his long-term memory had been affected by the surgery that had saved his life. He had looked at her like she was a stranger.

"I remember."

But for how long?

Because when she said she'd had her heart broken twice, she *meant* twice. First in their teens, when his memory had been affected—though it hadn't been as bad, and they'd managed to help him remember after just a week. Then in their twenties, a seizure and car accident revealing the tumor was back, and while the surgery had gotten rid of the cancer, it had also taken all of the love he'd had for her.

"How?" she breathed.

His gaze flicked beyond her. "Can I come in?"

Fanny's eyes slid closed. "Brandon," she whispered.

"I remember," he repeated.

"But for how long?" she said, out loud this time.

His inhale of breath was sharp, harsh amongst the quiet of the night, and she knew that he couldn't tell her. *No one* could promise he wouldn't get sick again, that she wouldn't be forgotten and broken and forced to pick up the pieces once more.

"Fan," he said, stepping toward her, the glass crunching under his shoes. "Can I come in? Please?"

She stumbled back a step, shook her head, her "No," more of a shaking exhale than an actual refusal.

He heard anyway.

And he stopped.

Because he was the kind of man who listened, who was respectful of boundaries. Who wouldn't force himself in where he wasn't welcome.

"Fan," he hissed, not moving, and the agony on his face had the claws inside her lashing out, striking deep enough to *hurt*.

Tears began falling, slipping out of the corners of her eyes. "No," she said again. Stronger this time.

Brandon didn't move.

She shut the door.

————

Fanny opened the front door of her house in the early hours of the following morning, having barely slept. The greasy food left to go bad; the wine and glass allowed to stain and litter the concrete of her porch.

Memories had tormented her all night long, had made it impossible for her to not see Brandon when her lids slid closed.

On the ice, playing travel hockey.

On the sidelines, cheering her on as she competed at increasingly bigger competitions.

Brushing back her hair and kissing her—her first—after she'd won Nationals.

Missing an important final so that he could watch her compete for gold.

Flowers and gentle touches, a room full of candles and giving her a narrow silver bracelet before they'd both lost their virginity.

The headaches. Passing out. The diagnosis. The surgery. The treatment. The—

She closed her eyes, focused on breathing in and out, but that didn't exactly help. Not after last night, not after Brandon had stroked her gently and told her to, "Breathe," in that husky voice of his. Because then she was thinking of his lush curls, those deep brown eyes, his strong shoulders, and roughened fingertips. He was the same and yet completely different.

A man.

Not a boy in the beginnings of adulthood.

And thank God the glass had stopped her from launching herself into his arms. He was a good person. She was glad he'd gotten better and that he looked so fit and healthy.

But she wasn't going there again.

Speaking of glass, she stepped forward, bringing the broom and dustpan with her. Then froze, eyes scouring the porch.

The glass was gone, not even the smallest sliver glittering in the overhead lights.

And the wine had been cleaned up, only a faint stain on her doormat telling her the entire interaction hadn't been a figment of her imagination.

"Brandon," she whispered, knowing instantly that he'd cleaned it.

Either that, or the magical wine fairies.

Snorting and feeling a little better now that her sarcasm had made a comeback, Fanny turned for the house and made short work of stowing the broom and dustpan before heading back out to her car.

Coffee.

Carbs.

Skating.

Another trifecta that had gotten her through the last decade.

Luckily, there was a Molly's around the corner, so she'd be able to obtain the first two easily enough, and the third was already on the agenda for the day.

She was running a power skating class that morning.

With seven-to-ten-year-olds. Heaven help her.

They'd be busy and talkative, and her head would be spinning by the time she was done, but she'd take the almost headache caused by her charges instead of the one that came from Brandon showing up on her front porch and making her *remember*.

"Carbs," she whispered. "Caffeine. STAT."

With that, she got into her car, hightailed it over to Molly's, managing to make it to the front door just as the Open sign flicked on, and snagging two apple cinnamon muffins—still warm and smelling absolutely delicious—along with a chocolate croissant—because when she said carbs, she *meant* carbs. Molly took one look at her and wordlessly made the large coffee Fanny had ordered an extra-large.

"Thanks," she said.

Molly just squeezed her hand before turning to help the next customer who'd come in.

Fanny stepped out onto the sidewalk, sucking down coffee and burning her mouth, but the caffeine rush was *so* worth it, and when she got to her car, she peeled back the wrapper of one of the muffins, consuming it so fast that she felt a bit like a snake. Just unhinge her jaw and let it slide down her throat.

"And now isn't *that* a pleasant thought?" she muttered, navigating out of the parking lot and onto the freeway, downing the other muffin without the least bit of guilt. She hadn't gotten her grease fest the night before. The least she owed herself was apple cinnamon deliciousness.

Along with chocolate croissant deliciousness.

Because that was also gone by the time she reached the rink.

Same as the coffee.

But at least she felt awake and somewhat better by the time she had her feet in her skates, the laces tied, the cold air biting at her nose and cheeks.

Home. This had always been and always would be *home*.

Cones and spray paint. Her clipboard, gloves, and beanie. The ice broken up with barriers and . . . kids. Talking and laughing, stumbling their way onto the ice, falling and getting up and tumbling into each other with a casual perseverance that reminded her of herself when she'd been their age. Well, that and the fact that they were so much closer to the ice than she was.

It hurt less when they fell that shorter distance.

Not that she was all that much taller, even now.

But a coach had to have her excuses, didn't she? Especially when the twins skittered toward her, nearly taking her out in their exuberance to show her *all* the hockey checks they'd learned in the two weeks since she'd seen them.

Grinning, she gently shoved them back, those claws in her

mind finally slipping free. She could breathe. She could laugh. She could . . . torture.

Muahaha.

Lifting her whistle to her lips, she blew a sharp trill to call the kids in.

And then she got down to torturing.

Two

BRANDON

His eyes felt gritty, and his finger still throbbed from the cut he'd gotten picking up the shards of glass from Fanny's porch.

But that wasn't what had kept him up the night before.

No, that was all Fanny.

Or at least, the expression on Fanny's face when she'd seen him, when he'd told her he remembered everything about them. Because it had been raw and hurt. *No*. She'd been anguished because *he'd* hurt her.

Too many times.

Cancer had taken too much from him. From *them*.

And still, he'd expected to walk up to her house, ring the bell, and for her to just fall into his arms.

Fucking idiot.

Sighing, he started for the front doors of Prestige Media Group, or PMG for short. He'd gotten a job here only recently, having made the switch from independent athlete representation to a firm. Not only did it pay better and the risks were lower—especially when the established company was the premier sports agency in the business—but his clients now had access to better perks than he could secure on his own.

Including Kaydon Lewis.

The former number one pick had recently been traded to the Gold. A good pickup for them because Kaydon had talent, even though he'd been battling some lingering injuries and hadn't yet lived up to the hype of being the first-round selection in the draft.

That would be different this season.

Brandon had seen that in the few pre-season skates the team had organized.

Which was how he'd stumbled upon Fanny. He hadn't known she worked for the Gold, hadn't known anything other than she'd moved to California all those years ago when he hadn't understood how important she was to him.

When the fucking cancer had taken that from him.

But fate had given him something back. Fanny on the ice when he'd gone to watch Kaydon, to make sure he wasn't pushing his recovery.

Brandon had . . . well, he didn't know what in the fuck all he'd done aside from standing there, mouth agape as he'd spotted Fanny on the other side of the glass, her dark hair pulled back into a ponytail, a light blue headband standing out sharply against the brown locks, glittering earrings dancing in her earlobes, legs and ass encased in tight black leggings.

A woman now.

And even more beautiful.

So he'd become a statue, soaking in every detail of her—her smile, the confident way she approached the players and nudged them this way or that, touching a knee through a shin guard, a hip through hockey pants, a shoulder through pads. He'd hated that she had her hands on other men, even knowing it was ridiculous for any number of reasons, not the least of which was the fact that it was her job and perhaps, the biggest being that he had no fucking claim over her and hadn't for nearly a decade.

He'd shoved down the jealousy, and instead, he had *seen*.

That she was good, that the guys respected her. That she knew her shit, even for Kaydon, who was new to the roster. She'd helped him through favoring that right knee, had pulled him aside and worked with him individually for a while.

Then she'd gone back to the team, running them through several drills that had the giants on the ice moaning and groaning.

By the end, the guys had dragged themselves into the locker room, and she'd all but skipped her way down to the hall that led to the offices of the practice facility, her ponytail bouncing behind her as she disappeared.

Not once had she looked his way.

So, he'd done some sleuthing.

And he'd found out where she lived (thanks to the IP address registration for her website).

Then had shown up on her porch like an asshole, obviously interrupting her evening in and making her hurt all over again and . . .

Being an asshole.

Fuck.

"Why do you have a sour lemon face?" Olivia—a VP at Prestige—asked, and he realized he'd been glaring at the front door to the business but hadn't gone through it. "The sponsorship deal with Kaydon giving you problems? I can reach out to my rep."

"No," he said, forcing himself to snap out of it. "I just didn't get much sleep last night."

She eyed him for a long moment before shifting forward and opening the door, holding it wide for him to pass through ahead of her. The light breeze whipped her black hair around her face as she stepped closer and asked softly, "Are you feeling okay?"

They—Olivia and Devon, the owner of Prestige—knew about his history.

Brandon had felt the need to be straight with them before they'd hired him on. He needed time off occasionally for doctor's appointments and checkups and though, up to this point, his scans had all come back clean, Brandon knew that might not always be the case.

And he didn't want to hide that.

"I'm good," he said. "Just a shitty night's sleep."

She nodded, studying his face for one more moment before turning toward the parking lot. "Let me know if that changes."

Now was his turn to do that.

At least to start nodding.

Because just as he'd started to incline his head, Devon Scott stormed up to the building, the former hockey player's body encased in an expensive suit, though the tie was loose around his neck and there appeared a be a Cheerio stuck to the collar of the crisp white shirt. "You will *not* believe what Becca did," he announced without any preamble.

Olivia whipped around, her eyes gleeful—she loved to gossip —as she clapped her hands together. "I thought you were going to stay home after lunch?"

"I *went* home—"

"And were apparently attacked by Cheerios?" she asked, brushing the collar of his shirt and tightening his tie.

Brandon bit back a chuckle.

Devon's face softened, the love he had for his toddler son evident. "Jasper was a little . . ."

"Don't talk bad about my godson," Olivia warned, lips tipping up at the corners. "He's a perfect angel, just like his Auntie Olivia."

This time Brandon couldn't hold back the chuckle, earning him a glare from Olivia and a smile in male solidarity from Devon. "What did Becca do?" he asked, trying to get Olivia's piercing blue eyes off him and back onto Dev, who was clearly more adept at handling her laser focus, if only because the other man had known her longer.

Devon sighed and thrust a hand through his hair. "You won't believe it."

Olivia grinned. "She made you sleep on the couch again because you snore?"

Dev scowled. "No."

"Hmm." Olivia tapped a finger to her chin. "Then are you mad because she had barely agreed to work for Prestige again before getting pregnant, having Jasper, and then decided not to come back and work for us—for *me*—again?"

"What?" A sharp shake of his head. "*No*," Dev said. "I'm fine with her working or not. I liked her here, even when she was working with you. It's just . . ." He trailed off, eyes going unfocused.

Olivia patted him on the shoulder. "That Bex cut you off from sex because you have an obsession with desktop fucking fantasies?"

"What?" Dev shook his head, his scowl deepening, though there might have been the slightest bit of red on his cheeks. "Where do you get these things?"

Olivia tapped her temple. "From the gloriousness of this giant brain." A beat. "And also because I'm friends with your wife."

Brandon snorted.

Dev continued shaking his head, kept scowling as he said, "Becca signed me up to be raffled off." He tossed up his hands. "I'm a prize for the Miner's Club charity event."

The Miner's Club was the Gold's charity, focused on providing sports opportunities for kids in the Bay Area, along with donating school supplies and funding after school activities for kids who either couldn't afford them or who didn't have safe places to be once the school day was done.

"That doesn't sound so bad," Olivia said. "I know a lot of men would like to be considered a prize."

"Would Cole"—Olivia's husband—"like being a prize?"

"Well," she said, waving a hand, "one could say he already is one. Both figuratively *and* literally."

"He's being raffled off, too?"

A nod.

Dev's scowl came back in full force, as though learning that piece of information meant that any hope of getting out of the event had now been dashed.

Olivia went on, "He's taking one winner up to the ranch for the day." Cole's ranch was another children's charity, introducing kids to the outdoors—hiking, swimming, horseback riding. All things that might not be readily available to children who lived in the city.

"The ranch." Dev made a face. "I'm a *date!*"

Brandon's brows lifted.

"So?" Olivia asked.

"*So?*" Dev's nostrils flared. "My own wife is setting me up on a date!"

Brandon's phone buzzed, a reminder that he needed to get moving.

"Oh Lord," Olivia sighed, threading her arm through Dev's. She met Brandon's eyes, him checking his phone apparently not having escaped her notice. "Run off while you can, young Jedi. I've got this one." She started to lead him back to his car. "Becca knows that you'll be a good prize. You'll raise lots of money and . . ."

Their voices began to fade, and Brandon found himself smiling.

Then he found himself trailing after them and offering, "Let Becca know that I'm happy to help out, too?"

Dev's eyes widened. "To take my place?"

Brandon shuddered. The only one he wanted to go on a date with was Fanny, and only if that meant he wasn't going to hurt her. The idea of entertaining some random man or woman for the evening, having to make small talk all while being uncertain of their expectations . . .

Well, he was hard-pressed to stifle his shudder for a second time.

"I . . . um..."

Olivia frantically shook her head, mouthing, "Don't do it."

"No," he said, "I was actually thinking that I could help in some other way."

Dev's shoulders fell. "Right." A beat. "Cool, thanks. I'll tell her."

Olivia patted his arm. "Your wife loves you. The date is a good thing. And if it really bothers you, just tell Becca you don't want to do it."

"You know I can't do that," he said. "The baby—" A sharp shake. "I don't want to stress her out and have something happen . . ."

Becca and Dev had struggled with infertility over the years, and Brandon knew she was only a few months along with their second baby. That alone nearly had him rescinding his refusal to take Dev's place. Olivia, apparently, knew that. She shook her head at him and made a shooing motion. "Go," she mouthed. "He's fine."

Hesitating for another moment, at least until his phone buzzed again, the reminder telling him he really *did* need to go otherwise he'd be late, Brandon slipped away and retreated to his car.

And drove away just as Olivia folded Devon into his, the other man still scowling.

But at least he was sans Cheerios.

———

He closed his eyes and held still as the noise rattled through the space around him.

Loud enough to make his ears ring and his jaw clench.

It was his yearly scan, and one would think he'd gotten used to the sound and claustrophobically small space by now, but he still hated MRIs with a passion, and just being in the narrow tube had sweat breaking out on his nape.

Slow, even breaths.

Not moving unless he wanted to repeat the whole damned thing.

Which, for the record, he didn't.

But being trapped in a white tube, magnets zipping all around him, was not his favorite place to be. Being still and quiet with no other distractions *also* wasn't his favorite place to be. That allowed him far too much time to think.

To remember.

When fuck, this whole shitty scenario began because he *couldn't* remember.

And now, he could only think of the bad things. Of the buzzing sound that had replaced words when he'd sat in that doctor's office and heard he had cancer the first time. His parents had been there then, still alive, and Fanny had been, too, her fingers finding his and holding tight when he'd received the news.

Her fingers had found his so many times over the years.

Just before he'd gone under for surgery the first time.

When he'd awoken and not remembered who she was, even though it was only for a week the first time. She'd still come every day, still held his hand.

She'd skipped school, snuck out from her house, stopped skating until he'd remembered and had forced her to return to the rink, to her training.

But even with school, with her skating, he'd never doubted that she was there for him.

Their friendship, begun at the rink, had grown into young love, and after he'd gotten better, they'd shared their first kiss, their first time making love, they'd spent every single day together, including him traveling to watch her bring home a silver medal on the world's stage. Then he'd gone to college while she'd performed on the pro tour circuit, and though the distance had been brutal, she'd been wrapping up her commitment, and he'd just graduated when he proposed.

She'd planned—*they'd* planned—everything. The venue. The food. Their honeymoon.

She'd tried on dresses, dresses he'd never gotten the opportunity to see her in.

They'd tasted cakes and couldn't wait to lay out on the beach together as newlyweds.

And then it had all gone to shit.

He'd made it all go to shit.

His eyes stung, throat burning, and he knew that he was seconds away from losing his shit in this fucking tube, the goddamn buzzing scratching over his skin. It was too small, too loud, too much stimulus for his overwrought brain.

He needed to get up, to get out, to—

His fingers twitched then his toes, and he clenched his jaw.

Don't move.

Don't move.

Don't—

Fuck it, he was going to move. He had to get out of here, had to—

The whirring stopped. "Mr. Cunningham?" the radiology tech's voice rolled through the small space. "Are you all right? Your heart rate has accelerated."

Fuck. *Fuck.*

He forced a deep breath, released it slowly. "Sorry," he rasped. "I must have dozed off there for a bit. Nightmare."

The tech laughed, and Brandon's throat burned. The prickling feeling didn't dissipate, but he forced his breathing to slow, to steady.

"I feel your pain," the tech said. "Good news is we're almost done here."

"Okay, thanks," he managed to squeeze out, even though the words were hardly decipherable.

The whirring picked up again, the tech didn't say anything else.

And Brandon slammed his eyes shut, pretending that he was anywhere but there.

THREE

FANNY

She was right about her head spinning by the time she got the kids off the ice, much later that afternoon.

Exhaustion had crept into every inch of her, and her toes were absolutely freezing . . . along with her fingers and her legs and her nose and her arms and—well, every part of her was frozen. She was ready to call it a day, probably should have called it a day about three classes ago. But her coach that typically did the afternoon lessons had looked a little peaky, so Fanny had sent her home.

She didn't mind . . . except for the whole freezing part.

She'd warm up. Eventually. And the exhaustion would help her sleep.

Plus, before she hit her bed, she'd have her wine and horror flick and carbs, take two.

After skating to the far side of the ice to snag the last cone—there always seemed to be one left behind—Fanny made her way off the rink. A perky, adorable redhead was waiting for her at the door to the ice, practically bouncing on her toes. She waved, nearly dislodged her glasses, and then immediately pushed them back up her nose. "Hey!" she called.

"Hi, Scarlett," Fanny called back, biting the inside of her cheek to hold in her smile.

"I wanted to talk to you."

"No kidding?" she asked dryly, coming to a stop before her.

Scarlett, the assistant publicist for the Gold, swatted her arm then backed up so Fanny could get off the ice, move to the bench, and pick up her skating bag. She rolled it toward the front of the rink, pushing through the doors that led into the warmer lobby area—thank God for that.

Step one of unfreezing.

Step two?

Resting her tired tootsies by sitting on the bench as she unlaced her skates. Scarlett plunked down next to her, talking a mile a minute. ". . . and so the raffle is going to be the big fundraising initiative for the year, and we need to raise enough to fund all the big projects, and our agenda this year is *huge*, and that's a lot of responsibility, and Rebecca wants me to—"

"Scar," Fanny interrupted, smiling at her friend. "You can save the hard sale for someone else." She bumped Scarlett's shoulder with her own. "I'm happy to help. Just tell me what you need me to do."

Scarlett beamed. "Can you donate some private lessons?"

Fan dried the blade of her skate, slapped on the guard, and tucked it into her bag. "Of course, I'll donate some. How many? Five?"

"Five would be awesome!" Scar's smile went somehow wider.

Fanny took off her other skate, dried it, and put it away as Scarlett kept talking about the raffle—Devon Scott—retired player and former member of the Sexiest Player of the Month club—would take a fan to dinner, Stefan Barie—their former captain—had offered a seat next to his for a home Gold game, Char Harris—the Gold's GM —was making herself available as a mentor. And all of that goodness would be followed by a silent auction with more items like tickets to Disneyland and wine tours of the North Bay. "Wouldn't my prize fit in better with those?" she asked when Scar finally took a breath.

Private lessons from a skating teacher hardly compared to the goodness of the others.

Her friend shook her head. "Um, no. A silver medalist giving free private lessons is a big prize."

"Except they can"—she swept her hand toward ice—"just come to the rink and sign up for a class."

Scar shrugged. "I'll give you that much, except that you don't teach too often anymore."

Not true exactly.

She did teach, but rarely instructed adults outside of the Gold roster. Maybe that was the draw?

Whatever the reason, Scar was emphasizing her silver medal and the private nature of the lessons—which was starting to sound a little more call girl and a little less instructor—and Fanny's strong suit wasn't selling people or spinning publicity or creating a great charity event. It was skating.

So, she let Scarlett run the show.

"Okay," she said during another pause in the one-sided conversation. "I'll do whatever you want."

Scar clapped her hands together. "I love it when people say that!"

Fanny snorted as she rolled her shoulders and stood. "I bet you do." She stifled a yawn. "Well, I should head home. I'm exhausted."

"Kids." Scarlett made a face.

And exes, she thought, struggling to keep her own expression neutral.

"But that's no excuse," Scar said. "Because you're not going home. You promised to go to dinner with Dani, Ethan, and me, and you're not flaking out this time, not just because of some kids."

"So says the woman who hardly has to deal with kids."

"So says the woman who is helping to run a charity *for* kids," Scar countered.

"*For* doesn't mean dealing with." Fanny chuckled at the expression of consternation on her friend's face. "But I really am tired. Do you mind if I flake?"

More consternation.

Crossed arms and a pouty bottom lip.

"No," Scar muttered, though that was very much a *yes.*

Fanny was immune to pouting. She'd had kids throw pretty much everything at her over the years—and that went for men and players, too. Because kids weren't the only ones with temper tantrums, though typically the ones she dealt with from the Gold were in jest.

Still, Scar's pouting in that moment had her reconsidering.

Not because of the stuck-out lip, but because of the prickling in Fanny's brain, the sudden knowledge that if she went home to her quiet house, to her cleaned-up front porch, to her wine and movie, that she wouldn't be able to keep her mind off Brandon. No matter how much popcorn she crammed down her throat. No matter how many carbs she consumed.

Maybe going to dinner would be better than being alone.

Scar's lip slid out a little further.

Maybe not.

Scar dropped her arms and pulled out the big guns. "We're going to Bobby's," she cajoled. "Mozzarella sticks, tacos, that weird panty-named drink that you love."

"A Panty Dropper?" Fanny sputtered. "I got that as a joke *one* time."

Scarlett nudged her with her elbow. "Well, maybe it's time for a second?"

It was the eyebrow waggle that did it. That and the fact that exhaustion meant she didn't have a lot of fight left in her.

Lie.

But sometimes a girl needed to lie to herself.

Plus, there were tacos on the menu.

"I know that face," Scar said. "It's the coming to Bobby's face."

Now she wanted to lie and say no all over again, just to wipe the smug expression off *Scarlett's* face. But . . . tacos and maybe she would go crazy and order a Panty Dropper, just to watch Dani blush all over again.

"Am I wrong?" Scar said when all Fanny did was glare at her.

"You're not wrong," Fanny said, ignoring the gleeful squeal as she grabbed the handle of her skate bag and started to roll it out of the lobby. Her car was parked out front, and when she got to the lot, she saw that Scar had taken the space right next to hers. "I'm surprised that you didn't block me in before I agreed to come with you."

Scar winked. "I had confidence in my skills of persuasion."

Laughing, Fanny just shook her head as she stuffed her bag in the trunk. "Want a ride?"

A nod from the girl with sparkling blue eyes. "You know how much I hate driving."

That her friend did. Not only did she hate it, but she was also terrible at it, having gotten into a number of smaller fender benders over the year or so she'd known Scarlett.

Mock-sighing, she hitched a thumb toward the passenger's side. "Get in, Trouble."

Scar frowned. "I don't *try* to be trouble, you know that, right?"

"Right," Fanny said, agreeing both because it was the truth—Scar didn't appear to seek out trouble, even *if* trouble seemed to follow in her wake everywhere she went (hell, it was a miracle Scar had parked next to her and Fan's car had remained unscathed)—but also agreeing because she really was hungry, and those tacos were calling her name.

Mmm.

Carne asada.

Maybe that was better than wine and solitude and slasher flicks.

She opened the door and sat down in the driver's seat, opening her mouth to ask Scarlett how work was going.

But she didn't get one word out before Scar blurted, "My brother's moving to town, and I want to give him your number. His name is Charlie, and he has pretty blue eyes, a great smile, and a stable job. Plus, he's got the perfect amount of squish."

Fanny's brows lifted, but she didn't get the chance to ask the question on the tip of her tongue (namely asking what was the perfect amount of squish) before Scar kept talking.

"He's huggable and good-looking and funny. Plus, he's single. He's the perfect Fanny material."

She'd hope so—the single part, anyway—if Scar was trying to set them up.

"I'm not really—"

She picked up Fanny's phone, plugging in the code to unlock the screen, and for a moment, Fanny regretted having shared the set of numbers that last time they'd ridden together. Then it had been to access a playlist; tonight it was to plug in Charlie's information.

Or at least, that was what Fanny assumed by Scar setting the cell back into the cupholder and leaning back in her seat. "There. Now you can call him and you two can meet up and you'll fall in love and then you'll have to be my sister and put up with me."

Heaven help her.

But she caught a glance of Scarlett's sparkling eyes, the utter joy and life and . . . found Scar's enthusiasm contagious.

At least enough to smile and say, "I don't know about the love part."

"But you'll call him?"

Fanny pressed her lips together to stifle the chuckle. Persistent meet trouble.

And Scar hadn't even pulled out the pout this time.

She drove out of the lot, navigated to the freeway, and found herself agreeing. "Yeah, Scar, I'll call him."

"And *that's* when Dani started blushing and swatting me, trying to shut me up," Scarlett said. "But I wouldn't be deterred. Madeline"—Blane, a defenseman, and Mandy's, the trainer for the Gold, oldest kiddo—"deserved that Tickle-Me Elmo, and I was going to die on that field to get it."

"And by *field,* Scar means the long, white aisles of Target," Dani said dryly.

Ethan was grinning, his arm around Dani's shoulders, his hand rubbing up and down her arm.

She'd had that.

She missed that.

Missed *Brandon.*

Swallowing hard, she took another long swallow of her Panty Dropper—her third? Fourth? *Fifth?* Honestly, she'd lost count, hadn't realized how hard it would hit her to see the diamond ring, the happiness on her friend's face, the obvious love between her and Ethan.

It wasn't like she hadn't seen them all lovey-dovey before. Of course, she had. Hell, she'd pushed them together, had helped Ethan select the ring.

But . . . Brandon.

She was raw and exhausted and . . . drunk.

So, she had that going for her.

Cool.

The server came around, refilling drinks. "You want another?" she asked Fanny.

The room was starting to spin at the edges, but Dani and Ethan were still in focus, so she nodded. Irresponsible? Yes. But Scar, who was drinking water, could drive her home—and hopefully not wreck her car in the process.

Solid plan.

Yes, that was the Panty Droppers talking.

She lifted her glass, and oh look, it was good she'd ordered another because it was empty. Still, she sucked down a few more drops, mostly the dredges of melted ice. When she plunked the glass back down on the table, her gaze caught on Ethan's.

And because he was still in focus even though hardly anything else was, she saw the concern on his face.

Fuck.

Scarlett was still talking, but he leaned closer to her and asked softly, "You okay?"

She slapped on her award-winning smile. The one that she'd once used with sponsors. The one that had given her enough cash to have a decent retirement savings *and* to start her business. "Just tired. Kids are monsters," she added with a chuckle that sounded forced, even to her own ears, when the concern didn't go away.

Scarlett chimed in. "Fanny was on the ice *all* day."

"And I couldn't even torture them by making them do ladder drills."

Ethan winced. "I hate ladder drills."

She smiled widely. "I like what they do to your endurance."

A grin. A shake of his head.

"Plus, you really hate the Umbrella." A drill she'd come up with that involved cones and a copious amount of edge work.

And one that Ethan, who struggled with using his outside edge on the right side effectively, really *really* hated.

Case in point, he shuddered. "I do," he muttered. "I do."

"You should make him do it anyway," Dani said with a smirk that was very un-Dani-like.

Fanny lifted her brows. "Torturing him not one day after the man gave you a giant ring?"

"Yup." The smirk widened.

Ethan clamped a hand to his chest, over his heart. "You wound me."

Dani snagged that hand, kissed the back of it. "I kid. I kid. You know I love you, and I only approve of Fanny's torturing because I get to reap the benefits of it on your body."

Scarlett cackled.

Fanny grinned, pretended to make a tick on her mental checklist. "Umbrella. Check. Ladders. Check."

Ethan groaned.

"Think of it like medicine, baby." Dani patted his cheek. "It's good for you."

Another groan.

They kept teasing Ethan, and he was a good sport about it. And she was glad she'd come, even despite the happiness radiating from the happy couple across the table making her teeth ache. They deserved that happy, and . . . she did, too.

For the first time in a long time, she thought that she did, too.

And—oh look, right on the tail of that uncomfortable thought, the one that had her throat squeezing tight, bile churning in her gut—her glass was empty again.

She signaled to the waitress for another.

"You're driving," she told Scarlett when her friend took a breath and Dani started teasing Ethan about how he'd cried at the movie they'd watched the previous weekend.

Scarlett glanced from the glass to Fanny's face. "You're not okay," she said.

Fanny sipped again. "No," she admitted. "But I'll get there." A beat. "I always do."

———

Later that night, Ethan took pity on Fanny (and her car and the risk Scar's driving might bring to it), and drove them back to the rink. They stopped long enough to drop Scarlett off at her sedan before heading to Fan's house.

Fanny was less drunk and more buzzed, even after having finished that last drink, mostly because Ethan had ordered another plate of mozzarella sticks and everyone knew that greasy cheese soaked up alcohol. Right. Stifling an inner snort as Ethan swung the car out of the parking lot, she knew that last couple of drinks were a mistake. Mostly because she was nowhere near sober enough to drive.

And because her drinking too much, her losing control was unusual, she knew that she had sparked Ethan's protective tendencies.

He wasn't her man, but she was Dani's friend and part of the Gold, and that meant she wouldn't put it past him to pull out his caveman proclivities, trying to ferret out what was wrong and then invariably solve whatever problem he discovered.

It would be sweet.

But unnecessary.

So, she headed him off before he could get that far.

"Dani told me that you're thinking about getting another master's degree?" She nudged his arm. "What? Need to prove you're the smartest one on the team all over again?"

A smile in her direction, though she knew that if it were light out, she would probably see his cheeks were slightly flushed, despite his cocky words that followed. "There's no need to prove that I'm the smartest one." A beat. "I already know I am."

She snorted, this time aloud. But she asked him about his studies, despite the arrogance.

One, because she was interested. Two, because talking about it would hopefully distract him from any concern she might have triggered.

He started telling her about his latest round of courses, and he had a soft, rumbling voice.

It was pleasant and warm and with the streetlights whizzing by outside the car windows, the soft hum of the engine, she found her lids growing heavy, her brain slowing down, her muscles growing slack.

Black slid up and slowly, inexorably dragged her under.

FOUR

BRANDON

He was sitting on the porch, outside a dark house.

Outside Fanny's dark house.

There was no movie noise this time. Nor was every light flicked on, illuminating the ground floor like it had been when he'd come last night.

It was quiet and still.

Where was she?

He knew it was wrong for him to be there, especially after her reaction the previous evening, but he'd gone home after his appointment, had sat in his own quiet and still condo, and had found it impossible to stay there.

The walls were closing in.

He'd gotten in his car, and he'd driven off, intending to just circle the block or the neighborhood in order to clear his head.

But invariably, he'd found himself on her street.

In front of her house.

On her porch.

And now . . . watching her walk up the path toward him in the arms of another man.

If he'd been in the right frame of mind, he would have recognized that man as a player for the Gold—Ethan something—who was madly in love with his girlfriend, now fiancé. If he'd been in the right frame of mind, he would have noticed that the hold was more steadying and not sexual.

But he wasn't in the right frame of mind.

And Fanny—*his* Fanny—was in the arms of someone who wasn't him.

He rose from the porch and stalked toward them. Fucking stupid that was, the man towered over him, was huge and built and could turn his puny ass at five-foot-eleven, with a runner's body (reason one why he never would have made it to the NHL, even though he had loved playing) instead of that of a freaking hockey player, into pulp. But he'd already established that he wasn't thinking.

"What the fuck are you doing?" he snapped.

Fanny's head shot up, surprised eyes meeting his, but the man with her reacted faster, tucking her behind him and stepping toward Brandon. "Back up."

Two words, icy cold as another car pulled up.

Another person—a woman this time—walked up the sidewalk. "Ethan?" she asked.

"Get back in the car, baby," Ethan said, "and take Fanny with you." He never took his eyes off Brandon. "I'd suggest that you leave. Immediately."

The woman who'd paused next to Fanny, took her arm. "Come on."

Fanny didn't move, just stared at him.

And Brandon, even though it was stupid to not be keeping an eye on the man, who was a freaking giant and who could destroy him, found he couldn't stop watching Fanny, couldn't stop himself from pleading with her with his gaze.

He just wanted to talk with her.

A hand on his shoulder, shaking him roughly. "Get in your car and go."

The woman had stopped trying to drag Fanny down the path and now stood between her man and Fanny, another layer of protection.

"Fan," he breathed. "Please. I just want to talk to you."

She inhaled sharply, dropping her chin to her chest. But she didn't reply.

"She doesn't want to talk to you. Go home," Ethan said. "Stay away. She'll call you if she wants—"

Brandon took a step forward. "I need—"

"I don't give a fuck what you need," Ethan growled. "It's past midnight. She doesn't want you here, and—"

"It's okay," Fanny said softly.

His heart thudded hard against his ribs, hope blossoming in his bloodstream.

The behemoth in front of him glanced back over his shoulder. "Fanny?"

"It's okay," she repeated. "He's safe—" A shake of her head. "He won't hurt me, and . . ." A sigh. "We do need to talk."

"You don't have to talk tonight," the woman said.

And was right.

It *was* after midnight, and he could see the dark circles under Fanny's eyes, even when the moonlight was the only illumination. He should go, should reach out at a more appropriate time and—

"I want to get it over with."

A sharp slice of pain across his middle had Brandon rocking back on his heels.

He deserved that. God, he deserved it.

The woman linked arms with Fanny. "Okay then, we'll stay and—"

"No." Fanny shook her head. "I've got this. You and Ethan should go." She dropped her arms, stepped toward Ethan, and kissed his cheek. "Thanks for having my back and for driving me home. But I'm okay."

"Sure?" he asked softly enough that it barely reached Brandon's ears.

"Sure."

"We'll talk about this tomorrow," the woman said.

"I know, Dani," Fanny murmured on another exhale, this one slow and shuddering and with far too much defeat in the words to suit him.

"You'll text me when he leaves?" Dani asked. "No matter the hour?"

"Yes." More defeat. More resignation.

Brandon almost relented then, not wanting to hurt her anymore.

But then the couple was leaving, and Fanny was brushing by him, telling him, "Come on," as she walked up onto the porch. "You know," she said after she'd unlocked the door and walked inside, leaving it open for him to follow, "I never tolerated the caveman jealousy bullshit when we were together, and I certainly won't tolerate it today as a grown woman who's in charge of her own life."

He sucked in a breath. "Fan."

She flicked on a light and turned toward him, brown eyes flashing. "You wanted to talk," she said. "So, we'll talk."

But she didn't start talking at that moment. Instead, she spun on her heel and strode from the hall, into a room he saw was the kitchen as she moved to the fridge and pulled out a bottle of wine.

His mouth moved before his brain. "Haven't you had enough?"

Dumbass.

Yes, in the light of the kitchen, he could see the dark circles that were only hinted at outside, but he'd also seen the flush on her cheeks, the slight glassiness of her eyes. She'd been drinking. That was why Ethan had driven her home then.

And he'd reacted . . . like an ass. Twice over.

Fuck.

She glared at him but didn't comment on his inane question. Just went to a cupboard and pulled down a glass, pouring a healthy amount of wine into the container. And didn't offer him any. Rightly so, of course. Then took a long swallow, squared her shoulders, and asked, "What do you want to discuss?"

Her tone made him feel like they were in a business meeting.

Or two strangers on the street talking about the weather.

Impersonal. A little cold.

Could he blame her? Fuck, no. He absolutely couldn't.

But also, he didn't really know where to start. They had so much history, and it was all twisted and tangled, barbed with thorns. He found himself saying the only thing that came to his mind. "I'm sorry," he whispered. "So damned sorry."

Silence.

Charged and thick enough that it threatened to choke him.

But it didn't choke Fanny. Instead, it seemed to unfreeze her. She put down her glass and crossed to him, her face gentling. "It's not your fault."

He startled when her fingers found his, when her eyes came up and locked with his own.

"I should be the one apologizing," she said. "I'm . . ." She trailed off, her gaze drifting over his shoulder. "It hurt a lot to lose you that way, but it was just a terrible situation. You didn't mean to hurt me. Life just . . . happened, and having you show up brought it all back."

He turned his palm over, laced their fingers together. "I'm the one being an asshole. I showed up on your porch without warning. I just . . . I remembered, and I wanted to find you immediately, but I didn't know how to find you. I just knew you'd come to California." He cleared his throat. "So when I did see you, when I found out where you lived, I couldn't stop myself from coming."

"How long?" she whispered. "How long ago did you remember?"

"I—" Brandon shook his head. "Almost a year ago. My . . ." He paused, not wanting to bring up the woman he'd fallen for before he'd remembered Fanny.

But she was too smart, too intuitive to not miss his hesitation.

"Angela, right?" Fanny murmured. "Her name is Angela. I—" She cleared her throat. "I heard you two got married. What happened?"

"We were together for five years before we got divorced. She's . . . she was too good for me, and even if I didn't know you on the surface, something beneath knew she wasn't you." He squeezed her hand. "She's remarried now and has a daughter, along with one on the way."

"Oh."

The silence fell again, only this time it didn't unstick her. Instead, she went still, her eyes unfocused and her mind very far away.

"I'm sorry," he said again.

"I've never been mad at you—" A shake of her head. "No, I'm not going to lie. I was hurt and then mad, and it was easier to hold on to the mad. Because holding on to my anger meant it was easier for me to make it your fault that you didn't love me enough rather than some shitty thing that just happened that neither of us could control." She blinked, and her eyes focused on his. "It made you the bad guy, and that was much easier to accept than me thinking . . ."

"Thinking what?" he asked when long moments went by without her finishing.

"That it was my fault," she whispered. "That there was something wrong with me, and that was why you didn't remember."

His heart twisted, rage and agony winding its way down his spine, making his free hand clench, his fingers twitch where they were intertwined with hers. He clamped down on the urge to clench there, too. Because it would hurt her.

Because it would hurt her *more*.

Instead, he inhaled slowly through his nose, exhaled just as gradually.

Then he unclenched his free hand, gently tipped her chin up so her eyes could meet his, and said, "Nothing is wrong with you."

Her throat worked on a painful-looking swallow. "Then why didn't you remember?"

Soft, soft words that he could barely hear.

But words that made his heart twist again, had fiery regret burning through his lips. This situation had been so fucked, so *absolutely* fucked, and there hadn't been anything either of them could do. "I don't know, sweetheart," he breathed, sliding his fingers to her hair and gently tugging her against him. "But I'm so, so sorry I didn't."

"I know," she whispered, as she came to him, as her body pressed to his.

It was . . . everything he'd remembered. The feel of her in his arms. The smell of her hair. The way she hugged him tightly and just . . . *fit.*

Right.

They were right.

He smoothed his hand down her hair, committing this moment to memory, wanting to burn it into the marrow of his bones, every neuron in his brain. "Can you ever forgive me?" he asked.

She squeezed his waist. "I forgave you a long time ago."

The next question was just *there*—bubbling up his throat, dancing on the tip of his tongue, ready to give voice to everything he'd dreamed about since all those memories of them had come crashing down.

But before he could ask it, before he could ask her to give him another chance, she spoke.

And what she said sent all of his hope crashing down.

"I forgave you," she murmured. "But I can't do this again." A shuddering breath. "I'm sorry, but I just . . . *can't.*"

———

He didn't know how he made it home.

He didn't know how he even left that kitchen.

Only that when Fanny had stared up at him, her eyes glistening with tears, her face drawn in sharp relief from the old pain, he'd known he couldn't argue.

He'd had to go, to leave her be.

Cursing, he pulled into his driveway and started to move into the garage, but a large box on his porch caught his eye. That hadn't been there when he'd left. Throwing his car into park, he got out and headed up the walkway.

It was huge.

The box, along with his disappointment.

And his understanding.

Which was the worst part. Because he got why Fanny couldn't take another chance on him, on them. He'd had a fulfilling relationship with Angela, while she'd been left alone, heartbroken, moving several states away from everything she'd ever known.

She'd had to start over.

He'd been in love with another woman.

Maybe he'd been kidding himself in thinking they could overcome the past. No, he *had* been kidding himself.

He hadn't been hurt.

Fanny couldn't just flip the switch and forget all of that.

"Fuck," he muttered, moving over to the box, and seeing the return label on the top of it had guilt scalding through him, all over again.

Angela.

It was from Angela.

His eyes slid closed, and he sighed.

Then he stepped back, returned to his car, and pulled into the garage, closing the door behind him. He moved into the house, flicking on lights as he walked through, making his way to the front door. Part of him wanted to leave the box on the porch and hope that someone would steal it. The rest of him knew he needed to know what was inside.

That was the piece prompting him to drag the box over the threshold.

And also the one that had him cutting through the tape and pulling open the flaps.

His breath caught at the note on top.

Somehow this came with me during the move. I thought you might need to see it. I'm so sorry I didn't realize what it was sooner.

—A

He removed the packing paper and froze, his fingers finding the soft blue fabric covering the album. She'd made this. *Fanny* had made this. The first time he'd lost his memory. She'd brought it to the hospital, and he'd flipped through it, and slowly, he'd begun to remember.

Fuck, why did the tumor have to be where it was?

Why couldn't he have lost something else? *Someone* else?

He could have lived without the memories of his teen years, his college years, if only he'd been able to keep those of Fanny. But instead, the tumor, the surgery to remove it, had obliterated them all, and even though he'd eventually remembered, first college, then high school, he hadn't regained the blank space that belonged to Fanny. Not until last year.

Would this box have made things different?

He pulled out the album, flipping through the pages, seeing the pictures of them. At prom. In the local pool with their damp arms wrapped around each other. Him holding her close, the tip of her nose pink from being in the rink for hours on end.

So many good times.

So much erased.

He set the album aside, saw the second one beneath, and knew his mom must have packed this up before he'd left the rehab facility, after he'd fallen for Angela, after Fanny had stopped coming around. Probably, she'd wanted to protect him, but part of him wondered what would have happened if he'd had access to this. Would he have remembered sooner?

The second album was filled with pictures of them as well, but it also had tickets and programs, from when he'd flown to watch her compete for gold, museum and movie receipts from their travels, a stub from sitting in the front row and watching her perform during the pro circuit. All interspersed with photographs, with memories.

With Fanny and their love and—

He closed the album and set it aside, seeing that the rest of the belongings weren't nearly as soul-crushing.

A few hockey trophies and medals, from before he'd been sick, before he'd quit playing. An old poster of a Lamborghini, one of some supermodel he couldn't remember the name of—and not from the brain cancer or the surgery, but just because that type of female hadn't interested him in a long time.

Not when he remembered Fanny.

The rest of the world ceased to exist when she was around.

He started to stack the trophies and medals back in the box, intending to throw them and the rest of the junk away, when he saw what he'd missed at first glance.

A small clay frame.

Fanny had made it when they'd first become best friends.

Before he'd fallen in love with her.

Though, he knew it was probably what had first sent him from that path of friendship on to one that led to love.

"God," he whispered, running his fingers along the sparkling pink and purple clay swirls. He'd known when she'd given it to him—her at thirteen, him so much older (at least to his teenage mind) at fifteen—that he should hate it on sight or be embarrassed. He'd been pretending to be a tough guy then. Into hockey and video games and girls, not pink and purple glittering swirls. But he'd loved this damn frame.

Because she'd made it for them.

Because of the picture she'd had printed and placed inside.

They'd been playing around on the ice, one of the few times

that happened because Fanny skating was serious business, and she didn't waste her precious ice time.

But that day, her coach had gotten a phone call and his team, which had been practicing on the other rink, had ended their session early. He'd walked by the ice and had started teasing her—as one did when they were a fifteen-year-old boy who liked a girl but didn't know what to do with those feelings. And she'd challenged him to a contest.

A skating contest.

He'd laughed, dismissed it.

She'd taunted, convinced him.

Then had proceeded to destroy his ass with a series of techniques that had him stumbling more often than staying upright, even without using those that required a toe-pick—something his skates didn't have.

He'd refused to concede.

Her tasks had become increasingly more difficult.

And then . . . she had caught him when he would have fallen. For a second, anyway, because even back then, he'd outweighed her significantly. They'd teetered on their blades, wobbling, then had collapsed to the ice where they'd sat there in stunned silence for one long moment before laughter erupted.

Her coach had snapped the picture.

He loved it. Then and now.

Their arms around each other. Smiles huge, faces turned toward one another as though they'd shared the best joke either of them had ever heard.

Even though his ass had been bruised the next day.

Because they became inseparable after that moment.

One interaction, one taunt, one smile, and his whole life had changed.

But wasn't that life? A series of small moments, each having a huge impact. A few minutes of teasing that had brought Fanny into his orbit. Several more in a doctor's office that brought them closer despite the struggles. The sound of crunching metal, of smashing glass to take it all away.

He carefully set the frame on the table, but it tipped over, and something fell off the back. He snagged it, eyes searching its surface in order to make sure it hadn't broken, then turned his attention to what had fallen from the back. It was a notebook he'd never seen before, and when he opened the cover and saw his mom's handwriting, his heart ached.

He turned the pages, getting lost in her words, in the things she'd written, and missing her all over again.

Sighing, he shut the notebook and carefully went through the rest of the box, making sure he didn't miss anything else that was important then dumped the trophies and medals back inside. He didn't need the reminders of his mediocre efforts on the ice, nor of what he'd never been able to go back to afterward.

Then he carefully slid the albums onto his bookshelf, making sure they would be out of the direct sunlight, that they wouldn't fall.

Yes, they'd stayed cooped up in this box for who knew how long, and yes, they'd made it across several states from his mom's place to the one he'd shared with Angela to Angela's *new* place to here. But though the belongings had been boxed up and thrust around, left unprotected, that didn't mean he couldn't treat them with care now.

And yes, maybe he knew that he was talking about Fanny now, and not the albums.

Both were still precious.

As was the frame, which he picked up and brought with him upstairs, staying by his side as he brushed his teeth and shoved his dirty clothes in the hamper. He held on to it as he crossed to his bed and slid beneath the covers, tugging them up and over him.

Only then did he release the frame, carefully propping it on his nightstand, staring at their happy faces as he let sleep sweep up and take him under, promising himself, the universe, fate, and whatever god, gods, or goddesses were out there that he'd bring that light back into Fanny's life again.

Even if it was the last thing he did.

FIVE

FANNY

"Now again, but on the inside edge."

Groans abounded.

Laughing, she rubbed her hands together gleefully, channeling her inner villain, before waving the guys off to get started on the drills. Her time with the team in group settings like this would be winding down as the Gold focused more on hockey than on exploiting fundamentals, even if skating was probably the most important fundamental out there.

Stupid hockey players thought things like stick handling and shooting were important.

Meh.

If they couldn't skate, they couldn't play.

At least, that's what she liked to tell herself.

It inflated her grand sense of self and gave her a nice ego stroking at the same time. Win-win. At least for her.

Grinning, she skated up to Kaydon before he could take off with his group, indicating the boards with a tilt of her head.

He followed her over.

"You're favoring your knee again," she said quietly.

Caramel eyes met hers, a muscle in Kaydon's brutally defined jaw clenched. But he didn't say anything.

"Want to tell me why?" she asked.

His nostrils flared. "It's fine."

She slanted a glance over her shoulder, saw that the guys were progressing with the drill rapidly, and knew that if she wanted to keep this private and between her and Kay, then she'd need to have the discussion quickly. "It's not fine," she told him, "and if you don't want me to pull rank, you're going to tell me what's going on with your knee."

His eyes narrowed. His shoulders rose and fell on a breath. "I pushed it during my workout yesterday. Nothing is injured. It's just sore."

Fanny studied him closely. "Hit the showers. Check in with Mandy before you leave. Then come and see me the day after tomorrow. We'll work through the sore properly."

He opened his mouth.

"Kay," she said, placing a hand on his—or over his glove, anyway, "you're on the Gold, now. That means that you're not just a player or an asset. You're part of our family, and we take care of our family." She patted lightly. "It won't help anyone, least of all you, if you push your recovery so much that you can't play. We want you with us, but we don't want you to kill yourself getting there."

His lips pressed flat. "Right."

She'd heard rumors of the team he'd played with before, the drama and bullshit in the locker room, between the board and the players, the way everyone had turned on each other. Kay was new here, and she understood that he wouldn't necessarily believe the fluffy-puppy-dog-everything-is-rainbows approach that the Gold organization took. She hadn't at first. Until she'd legitimately seen that management cared for the players and made decisions based on their well-being and not how much they could squeeze out of them.

It would take Kaydon time to believe that.

But she wasn't going to let him fuck up his recovery until then.

"Do I need to pull rank?" she asked archly, when he didn't respond. "Either that or I can add some Elephants"—his most hated drill—"when you meet me."

Finally, his eyes seemed to melt, to soften, and one side of his lush mouth tipped up. "Ethan is right. You really are a monster in a tiny, sparkly package."

She grinned, swept a hand over the—yes, *sparkly*—logo on the custom shirt Brit had made for her. It went with her earrings (glittery pineapples today) and the bedazzled gloves that she wore. A woman had to take her happiness where she could find it, and sometimes that meant sparkles. Other times it meant wine and horror movies. Po-tay-toe. Po-tah-toe. She watched the guys finishing up and skating over to her one by one, knowing they could hear her. "It's good you know my inner colors. It'll save me the trouble of breaking your spirit later."

Kaydon scowled, though his eyes were dancing. "Like taming a horse?"

She considered that. "Or convincing a scared little kitten to come out from beneath the couch so I can pet him."

Silence.

Then the guys started busting up. Even Kay shook his head and smiled.

"So, Kitten," she teased. "You going to follow my orders?"

Max nudged Coop, who grinned and nudged Blane, who started to nudge Brit, but she sidled away, hissing, "Yeah, I heard. I don't need the elbow."

"Heard what?" Ethan asked.

"Kitten," Logan said, shoving back a hunk of brown hair that had slipped beneath his helmet.

Ethan's smile was slow and sexy and predatory. "Kitten," he agreed.

Fanny winced, glanced up at Kay. "Sorry?" Her voice pitched up on the end, making it more question than statement, and her apology was further ruined when she couldn't stop the laughter from bubbling up her throat.

"Monster," he repeated. But his lips were twitching, and he nudged her hip with his. "See you in two days?"

She nodded.

Kay headed for the door that led off the ice.

"Bye, Kitten," Max called.

The guys cackled.

Fanny winced again, though she couldn't stop her laughter again when Kaydon flipped them all off, his fingers looking like giant . . . marshmallows? No, that wasn't right. But anyway, it looked a little strange to be receiving the bird that was wrapped up in a bulky hockey glove.

"All right, you punks," she told them. "Because of you torturing poor Kaydon, I'm going to torture you all." She gave them a beatific smile in response to their moaning.

"You came up with the name," Max muttered.

"Just because we're going to keep using it," Coop added.

"Doesn't mean you need to torture us," Blane finished.

"Torture away!" Brit said.

The guys had been nodding in agreement. Until Brit.

Then they scowled. And Fanny rubbed her hands together again. "Okay, here's my proposition. I either give you all one more drill or . . ." She deliberately trailed off, almost laughing again when they all leaned in. "Or," she said again, even slower, "Brit takes you on a run."

"Run!" Brit shouted.

"Skate," everyone else yelled. Mainly because no matter how much they complained about Fanny's "torture," Brit taking them all on a run was the worst form of punishment they could imagine.

"Hmm." Fanny tapped a finger to her lips. "I think I heard run."

Ethan narrowed his eyes.

She grinned.

"All right. Fine. Umbrella. Three times on both feet"—Ethan slumped and Brit pouted—"and then our last group session of the preseason will be complete."

Whoops went up.

"Rude," she teased. "Maybe I need to schedule extra one-on-ones?"

Coop tugged her ponytail as he skated by. "You are small and shiny but equally as feisty."

"And mighty," Max added.

"And evil." Ethan.

"That doesn't rhyme," Max grumbled.

"Then evil-y," Ethan said. "Better?"

Max nodded. "Yup."

Shaking her head, Fanny skated to the boards, blew her whistle, and then focused her attention on the guys as they moved through the drill, making note on her clipboard of a few things some of the guys had to work on. But they were looking pretty damned good.

Not to pat herself on the back.

But . . . she patted herself on the back.

This was going to be a good season. She could feel it in her sparkly, evil bones.

————

The guys had cleared the ice, snagging the cones and tires she'd used during the session.

They were neater than the kids.

Or perhaps, better trained.

Or perhaps not, she realized just before she stepped off the rink, spying a small tire that had been left behind in the shuffle. Smothering a grin, she skated to the corner, scooped it up, and moved to the opposite side of the ice, where there was a storage unit for equipment.

She'd just tossed the tire inside when her nape prickled.

She looked up, and it was like some inner detector knew who it was and where *he* was. Where Brandon was.

By her skate bag.

Probably because he knew she would be trapped, would have to take off her skates at some point. She couldn't exactly drive home in them now, could she? Plus, she'd fuck up her edges.

He shifted from foot to foot, clearly uncomfortable.

The feeling was mutual.

But he didn't move away, even as she girded her loins and walked over to him. "Brandon," she said, proud that her voice was neutral. She'd meant what she'd told him the night before. She had forgiven him long ago, but that forgiveness didn't mean they could go back.

She couldn't welcome him back into her life. Couldn't risk it.

"Hey, Fan," he said softly, his voice sliding over her skin and making her shiver.

No. That was the cold air of the rink making her shiver. Not Brandon, nor his slightly raspy, all-too-sexy voice.

"I—" She broke off, cleared her throat. "What are you doing here?"

He held up a manila envelope. "Just had some paperwork for Kaydon."

Her brows drew together. "For Kay? Why?"

Brandon's brown eyes were warm on hers. "I'm his agent."

Surprise trickled through her, and yet she knew that it wasn't warranted. He'd gone to school for sports management, teasing that she would be his first client. Those plans had been derailed by the discovery of his cancer returning and his surgery, but of course, he'd found his way back to it.

And to me, her mind whispered.

Swallowing hard against the panic, and maybe the slightest bit of longing that thought invoked, she smiled. "That's great," she said, reaching out and squeezing his arm before she could stop herself. Sparks shot up her fingers, warmth coiling in her abdomen. "I'm so happy for you. Do you work for Prestige then?" she asked, knowing they represented a good chunk of the Gold roster.

Brandon nodded. "I brought my clients over and joined with them when I moved out here."

Speaking of which . . . why *had* he moved out here?

Was it for her? Or some other reason. Or—

"I didn't," he said quietly. "If I'd known where you were involved with the Gold, I would have come for sure. But I didn't."

Fanny's lungs seized. He would have come?

"Right after Kaydon was picked up by the Gold, I ended up running into Devon Scott at a conference. He wined and dined me"—a grin—"and convinced me to move over to Prestige. Luckily, my clients all saw it as a net benefit, so I'm pretty much doing the same thing I was before, just in a nicer office and in a better climate."

Her lips twitched. "No more snowy winters."

"Exactly."

Quiet descended, or at least it descended between them. The rink around them was noisy. The sound of the Zamboni cutting the ice echoing through the space, along with that of the kids who'd gathered on the opposite side, who were getting ready for practice. God, she loved this space. The noise, the smell, the cool air. Lucky for her, she supposed, considering she spent the majority of her time here, either with the guys or with her classes and clinics.

His eyes flicked over her shoulder, and she bit her lip. "I should let you go. Kaydon should be in the training suite—"

"Is he okay?" Brandon asked, concern whipping across his face.

"He's fine." She squeezed his hand again. "I noticed he was favoring that knee again, and he told me he just overdid it at a workout. I strong-armed"—a shrug when he glanced up at her—"or well, I *strongly encouraged* him to see Mandy."

"I'd wondered why he headed off early."

"You watched the session?"

He rocked back on his heels, studying her face, something flashing across his eyes that she couldn't decipher. "You're really good with them."

She inhaled, warmth blossoming in her stomach, spreading out to her fingertips. "They're good guys."

A nod.

More quiet.

Then he reached for her.

And for a moment, she didn't know what she wanted—to lean in and let him touch, to skitter back and run like her hair was on fire, to . . .

He held up a notebook.

Oh. *Oh.* He wasn't reaching for her. He was . . . trying to give her something.

Right.

"My mom," he said, and she immediately stepped back. That hurt, too. Because Brandon's mom had been wonderful. Sweet and funny and loving. Fanny's own parents were fine, albeit more than a little detached. She knew that they cared about her, but her parents were also very into their own lives. Her mom had a busy career, even now that she'd reached retirement age, and her dad had always been more interested in building his cars than her.

Skating and glittering skating outfits, new laces and music for routines hadn't appealed to him.

Nor to her mom.

They'd thrown money at Fanny's hobby, and that had been more than lots of other people had, so Fan knew she was lucky. It was just . . . she had traveled more with Sandy, her coach, than her own parents.

Until she'd gotten together with Brandon.

Then his parents had come to every competition they could, sitting beside Brandon in the stands. She'd had a support system she hadn't ever expected to have, and she really missed Grace. And Jeff. Brandon's dad had been a good guy, too.

She remembered one time when he'd helped Sandy track

down permission to a piece of music so Fanny could use it for her long program.

Her own parents would have just told her—*had* just told her —to pick another song.

So the hole after losing Brandon had been big and threefold. It hadn't felt right to keep in contact when he was trying to build a life with Angela. And, if she was being truthful, it would have been too painful to talk with them, knowing that Brandon was a subject they couldn't broach.

Or at least, couldn't broach without it hurting too damned much.

"My mom," he said again, not moving toward her, but still holding up the little black book, "wrote in this. I think she meant for you to have it."

"Brandon," Fanny began. "I can't. That belongs to you." She swallowed. "You should keep it, especially—"

"I want you to take it. You should—"

"All good, Fanny?"

Jumping, she glanced over to see that Dani had walked up, suspicion drawing the lines of her face into sharp relief.

"I'm good," she said and straightened her shoulders, lifting her chin, her tone going almost brusquely professional. "This is Brandon, my ex. It turns out he's Kaydon's agent and is working for Prestige Media Group."

Dani's brows climbed up her face. "Hi, Brandon." Her tone was icy.

"It's nice to meet you, Dani. I'd like to apologize for my behavior last night." His gaze came to Fanny's, voice gentling and eliminating all that brusque professional distance in a heartbeat. "To you, as well. I was out of line showing up like that."

She nodded. "It's okay."

Dani huffed and narrowed her eyes, none of the shy woman who'd she'd been before Ethan. There was fire in her that was no longer banked, and it was fucking fabulous to see. "It's not okay," she snapped. "You don't just show up being all combative. You call first, and if Fanny wants to see you, then you come." More eye narrowing, this time accompanied by some poking in the chest—Brandon's chest. "And you definitely leave the asshole attitude at home."

Fanny clasped her friend's hand, tugged her back, fighting a smile.

Because this was her shy, uncomfortable in social situations friend. This was *Dani* who was so damned quiet and jumpy until Ethan, until . . . herself. Because her transformation wasn't all because of another person. It was from Dani herself. She'd fought hard to get beyond her insecurities, had embraced the wealth of strength inside her heart and soul.

Ethan had just been the whipped cream and cherry—or perhaps, the push to take that first step.

"I promise I will leave the asshole at home," Brandon said, and though his tone was even, his eyes had mirth creeping in on their edges.

It didn't escape Fanny's notice that he hadn't promised to stay away or call first.

Just to leave the asshole at home.

Hmm.

"Good." Dani turned to Fanny. "Can I talk to you privately?"

"I—" Her gaze flicked to Brandon's.

"Go ahead," he said. "I need to go speak to Kay, anyway." He sucked in a breath, released it. "I'll . . . see you around sometime."

He turned away, and Dani drew her to the side. "Seriously, are you okay? Why is he here, and . . ." She began peppering Fanny with questions.

Questions which she deflected.

With promises to confess all soon.

Thankfully, that was enough to satisfy her friend for the moment, so the topic turned to the charity raffle and everything that was going to go into it. There were a lot of moving parts, and it would be a good event, but it was also big and complicated, so by the time she said goodbye to Dani and sat down to take off her skates, a fair amount of time had passed.

Enough time, she realized as she unzipped her skating bag, for Brandon to have performed a little bit of mischief.

The notebook was tucked inside.

The man was nowhere to be seen.

But the mischief was better than the asshole.

And Fanny had learned to take her victories where she could find them.

SIX

BRANDON

A knock on the door signaled the harbinger of darkness.

Well, either that or just his doctor.

Dr. Lyon was his new oncologist. He might have stayed with his previous one, even after having moved a couple of states away, but Dr. Philips had retired and had recommended Dr. Lyon, whose practice was conveniently located only a couple of miles away from Prestige's office.

Dr. Lyon was a petite brunette with a penchant for chunky necklaces and slacks paired with brightly patterned blouses.

After the perfunctory knock, she opened the door and stepped inside, closing it behind her with one hand, the other clasping a tablet. She glanced up, smiled. "It's nice to see you again, Brandon. How have you been feeling? Any changes?"

Always, his gut clenched when beginning this line of inquiry, even though he'd been feeling fine, even though nothing had changed, at least nothing that he could pinpoint anyway.

And that, the fear that something might be growing, but he couldn't feel it, never went away.

"No," he said. "No headaches or dizziness or nausea."

"Any more memories coming back?" They'd discussed the final return during their initial consultation when Brandon had first moved to California.

He shook his head.

"Anything lost?" she asked then pressed her lips flat. "Or rather, has anyone around you mentioned anything you can't remember?"

"No."

His memory hadn't been like that. The cancer itself had caused seizures and headaches, but it was always the treatment, the surgery that had been even more devastating, scooping out parts of him . . . or damaging them, anyway, leaving those pieces to heal so fucking slowly.

"Good. Good." She sank onto the edge of her desk and set the tablet in a holder, nodding at a large monitor on the wall as she plugged in a cord. "Your MRI has been viewed by the radiologist—"

His stomach twisted.

"—and everything is clear. There's absolutely nothing on the scans that indicate any return of cancer in your brain or anywhere else in your body."

He released a breath and was finally able to spare a thought for wondering why she'd asked him into her office. Usually, he just received a phone call with his results, and while part of him had been hoping it was just because this was his first checkup with Dr. Lyon, deep down he'd been worried they had found something.

And what that might mean.

"You have ten years of clear scans. Ten years free of cancer." She reached for his hand and squeezed it lightly. "In my medical opinion, I would consider you cured." Straightening, she smiled slightly as she pulled her hand back. "I wanted to make sure you understood that. You're healthy and young. You can have a full life." Her voice softened. "In case the specter of the cancer returning has been hanging over you."

How could it not?

But he appreciated what she was doing. What she was saying.

"Thank you."

"There's no reason for you to think the cancer will come back," she went on. "We'll continue with our yearly scans, because I think that will give you some further peace of mind"—she paused and glanced at him, so he nodded—"but I want you going out there and living your life without worrying about it. That worry will be my job. Let me shoulder that burden. You just . . . live."

He swallowed hard, his eyes shining.

Maybe it was presumptuous of her, because he didn't ever think the worry would one hundred percent go away, but it lightened something inside of him to hear those words, loosened some tension he hadn't even registered carrying.

Because it had been there for so long.

"Thank you," he said.

She squeezed his hand and straightened again. "You reach out to me at any time with any concerns, any changes no matter how small," she said. "But push me and this office and the scans out of your mind." She laughed. "Pretend I'm the boring mismatched sock, the one you forget about but never throw away."

He chuckled.

She grinned. "There, but forgotten is what I prefer. Or at least that's what I tell my single self." A wink.

Now he was laughing. In a doctor's office. Something he hadn't thought was possible, and Dr. Lyon joined in, too, her tinkling laughter drifting through the air, punctuating the conversation as she made sure he didn't have any other concerns or matters to discuss. Then she made her way to the door, smiling and waving before slipping out into the hall, and Brandon thought that if he wasn't hopelessly in love with Fanny, single Dr. Lyon would have been exactly the type of woman he could fall for.

But he was in love with Fanny.

Since that moment on the ice, *her* laughter coating his skin, *her* smile lighting up his soul nearly two decades before.

And now, he was deemed cured.

Now he had something he could give her, some reassurances where there hadn't been any before.

Now he could promise to be there and mean it, to not forget her, to be there for her exactly as she deserved.

Now he could finally give her everything.

He was grinning as he strode out of that doctor's office.

Hope.

That was what Dr. Lyon had given him.

And it felt damned good.

———

He tossed and turned, even despite going back to the office after his appointment and working on several contract offers, staying well past nine when the cleaning crew had come in.

The sound of the vacuum running had chased him from behind his desk, knowing he wouldn't be able to concentrate.

Not so much because of the noise.

But because the bubble of his concentration had been broken, and his thoughts had begun swirling about what the doctor had told him, and around Fanny and if he should tell her (how could he *not* tell her?). Wondering if it might make a difference because he understood that she needed to protect herself from being hurt again, and if he *did* tell her, how he could ask her to take a risk.

He wasn't the one who'd been devastated.

Sure he'd been sick, but he'd found love and happiness.

And Fanny . . . had been forgotten.

Sighing, he tossed back the blankets and went out the sliding glass door in his bedroom. It led to the back yard, darkened and full of shadows, the moonlight diffused by the thick covering of fog. The air was cool enough to have goose bumps prickling on his skin, but he didn't put on any clothes or shoes as he moved across the porch and leaned on the railing, staring up at the sky.

The fog curled and shifted as it trailed over him, giving occasional glimpses of the black sky, the twinkling stars, the nearly-full moon.

He had a decision to make.

No. He was kidding himself by thinking that. He'd made the decision already, the moment he'd first seen Fanny again, had watched her work her magic on the ice.

He wanted to rekindle things with her.

He wanted to build a life with Fanny.

He wanted to give her the white dress, the fantasy of happily ever after.

But what if she didn't want that? She'd told him that she'd forgiven him, made it perfectly clear that he was a risk she wasn't willing to take. Except, that was before Dr. Lyon had said he was cured. That would change things, right? That would make a difference and—

Maybe it wouldn't matter.

Because while Dr. Lyon had said she didn't think the cancer would come back, she also couldn't promise him with one hundred percent certainty that it wouldn't.

And maybe that wouldn't be enough for Fanny.

Rage whipped through him suddenly with a severity that sucked the breath out of him as his hands clenched into fists, as every muscle in his body went taut. "So what?" he snapped, well aware that he was talking to himself or the shadows or the fucking moon hiding behind the fog. "You're just going to give up? You're not going to fight for her?"

That was bullshit.

He'd almost died. Twice. He'd been through six rounds of chemo. Radiation. Had two major surgeries and the physical therapy.

And *now* was the moment he was going to give up?

"Seriously?" he muttered, banging his fist on the railing. "Now?"

Fuck that.

"Fuck *that*," he said out loud.

He had to fight for her. He'd survived. He remembered. He loved her.

Fuck, that *had* to be enough.

It had to.

His heart was pounding from confirming the decision, his hands still clenched, his muscles still tight, but just thinking that he was going to fight for her, just making that promise *to* fight for her had rightness settling over him like it was a second skin.

He'd never once given up on anything. Surviving. Getting healthy again. Finishing his degree. Starting his business. Even his marriage.

Angela had been the one to file the papers.

Not because he had been clueless to their problems or the fact that they'd grown apart and were heading in separate directions.

But because he *didn't* give up, and without remembering Fanny, he would have continued fighting for her. If he had remembered when he'd been with Angela, that would have brought a whole set of different complications. But he hadn't, so he didn't need to think himself in circles worrying about it. The point was, he'd fought for Angela and while he still loved his ex-wife (albeit that love was strictly platonic now and had been for years), that love paled in comparison to what he felt for Fanny.

The first woman to own his heart and soul.

The woman who still held it today.

How could he give up on her?

"I can't," he said, head tilted up to the sky.

It was as simple as that.

No matter the hurdles they still had to overcome.

He wouldn't give up on Fanny, wouldn't give up on their future, wouldn't give up on trying to build something unbreakable between them, on filling in the holes his illness had carved, on erasing the sadness in her eyes, her soul, her heart.

A few steps brought him back inside, a few more to his closet where he tugged on a pair of jeans and a shirt, pulled on socks and shoes before walking from the bedroom.

Past the pink and purple frame.

Down the stairs and to the garage.

He needed to see her car in her driveway, needed to make sure that she was home and safe.

He needed to see her house, even if he couldn't see *her*.

Because he wouldn't bang on her door, wouldn't barge into her house. He was going to win her over as she deserved—slowly and gently and with plenty of love and care. As promised, he'd leave the asshole at home.

He'd just get a glimpse of her car, her house, maybe even Fanny herself.

Then he'd come back home and plan.

SEVEN

FANNY

"What do you think of this one?" Scarlett asked, spinning in a circle, the emerald skirt flaring out.

"It's gorgeous," Fanny said, standing up from the chair she'd been waiting in and rubbing the material between thumb and forefinger. It was silky and cool and the perfect color to match the creaminess of Scarlett's skin, to highlight the deep red of her hair. "You're going to knock him dead."

Scar winced. "Let's not use that turn of phrase."

"Why not?" she asked, reaching up and straightening the straps. "You're beautiful in it," she said, glancing into the mirror and meeting her friend's eyes.

"Thank you." Scar reached up and covered Fanny's hand. "But no knocking them dead. We don't need to tempt fate, not when it comes to me and my thundercloud of trouble. You give voice to it, and it might happen, and"—she made a face—"I might not get laid."

Fanny laughed, smoothing the material of the straps before stepping back. "Well, we definitely don't want to get in the way of you and several delicious orgasms."

"No, we don't."

She mimed zipping her lips shut. "Your secret is safe with me."

"Not sure it's a secret," Scar murmured, reaching down and checking the price tag, a frown dragging her red brows together. "Disaster follows in my wake, even without me trying."

"It wasn't your fault that the stick rack collapsed."

They were shopping for Scar's date, partly because Scar *had* a date and partly because Scar had needed a little retail therapy after an eventful day at the rink. They'd been shooting some publicity photos for the website and social media when trouble had struck.

At least, that was what Scar believed.

Brit had assured Fanny that Scarlett hadn't been anywhere near the equipment when the rack had fallen apart, scattering sticks every which way and making everyone in the vicinity jump, but Scar was convinced it was her bad juju and that it boded poorly for her date and maybe her future with the Gold.

Nonsense.

Because not only was Scar great at her job, but any man would be lucky to be dating her friend.

So when Fanny had gotten off the ice and seen her friend with a forced smile, she'd endeavored to find out what had happened, then to make it her mission to make her feel better.

A new dress was the first part of that.

Next would be shoes and undies.

And yes, she understood that it was ridiculous for her to call them undies. But *c'est la vie* and all that.

The point was that she was going to help Scar feel good, take her mind off the so-called bad juju and trouble that followed in her wake, and then she'd point her in the direction of her date and hope that she got some orgasms.

Oh, and maybe some fun and good conversation and a man who saw Scar for the lovely person she was.

That, too.

"It was my fault," Scar muttered. "I bumped into it when I

first went into the room to get everything set up this morning and it—"

"And it decided to randomly fall apart hours later?" Fanny asked. "After many other people used it throughout the day?"

Scar ran her hands over the skirt and made a face at her in the mirror. "Fine. Be logical, why don't you?"

Fanny smiled. "I will." A beat. "Are you getting the dress?"

Scar tilted her head from side to side, the red waves of her hair sliding from shoulder to shoulder. "Yes," she said with a decisive nod. "I like it and even though it is way too much money for a freaking scrap of fabric"—this was true, the dress revealed more skin than it covered—"it's sexy and looks amazing on me, and that's good enough for me."

"As it should be." Fan nodded to the curtain. "Get changed. Let's get some stuff to go with that fabulous dress."

"Lace things?" Scar asked.

"If that's what you want," Fanny replied, hiding a smile, glad that her friend was finally getting on board with her plan.

"And shoes?"

"Duh."

Scar grinned. "What about you?" she asked as she slipped back behind the curtain to take off the dress. "Are you going to buy any lacy things for that ex of yours?"

Fanny's throat spasmed for a moment before she managed to get a reply out. Of course Dani had dished about Brandon . . . to *everyone*. The Gold gossip train was notorious and efficient, as thus Fanny had been getting questions about "the ex" from everyone—players to support staff to the front office—that entire day. But not from Scar, apparently, who had just been waiting for her moment to pounce.

"I think you already answered your own question," she muttered. "He's my ex for a reason. No lace for him."

Scar poked her head out from behind the curtain, her brows lifted.

"What?" Fanny asked.

"Nothing." Scar disappeared again, the curtain fluttering. She reappeared a moment later, the dress back on the hanger and all the others she'd tried on before the emerald one in her other hand.

Fan moved forward and took the rejects. "Let's go to shoes first." She hung them on the rack of go-backs, started for the exit of the dressing rooms. "I think I saw a pair that will look perfect—"

"Who is Brandon, really?" Scar asked, catching her arm. "Because he doesn't look at you like you're an ex."

"How does he look at me?"

"Like you're something he's desperate for." She clicked her teeth together, nom-style. "Like he wants to eat you up."

Franny inhaled sharply, shook her head. "I-I can't. It's—"

"Complicated?" Scarlett asked, tugging her toward the displays of shoes. "Everything that's really good in life is complicated."

"This is really complicated, Scar. Not just normal complicated."

"Why?"

This wasn't really a conversation she wanted to have in the middle of a department store. Okay, fine. This wasn't a story she wanted to share *ever*. But also . . . she *wanted* to talk about it. She wanted it off her chest, for the pain and longing to stop eating at her. She wanted her friend to understand, wanted *someone* to understand.

So, as they wandered through high heels, she told Scarlett everything about Brandon—how their friendship began at thirteen and fifteen, him becoming her first love when she'd turned fourteen and he'd been sixteen, the cancer, and that horrible week of him not recognizing her, not remembering. She told her friend how amazing it had been when he'd gone into remission, how his family had become hers and supported her during her skating career, how they'd made long distance work despite it not working for so many others. Her voice shook when she told her about the seizure when he'd been driving and how they'd discovered the cancer had come back, the surgery, him waking up and not knowing her.

"I tried for months," she whispered. "I tried everything. I brought out albums of us, made new ones with all of the things we did together, hoping that he would see something and it would spark his memories. I made playlists and brought him on field trips to our favorite places. I baked for him. I put on our favorite movies and TV shows." Her eyes burned. "I spent months and *months* doing that, along with accompanying him to his physical therapy, his checkups. I spent hours with him, all while loving him desperately, and he only looked at me like I was an acquaintance or a new friend he barely tolerated because I was so close to his parents." A sigh. "It never grew into anything, and I could have handled him not remembering me, could have put all my new energy into building a new future together, but . . . he didn't love me." She sniffed and wiped a tear that threatened to leak from the corner of her eye. "And then I watched him fall for his infusion nurse. I saw him light up for her every single time he went in for treatment, when they happened to run into each other when he was there for a different appointment. There was chemistry and potential, and I saw what it did to him to pretend those feelings weren't there."

"Oh, Fan."

Swallowing hard, she kept her focus on her hands. "Because even though he didn't love me like I loved him, he was still a nice guy and didn't want to hurt my feelings." She closed her eyes. "I waited six months. And then I rejoined the pro tour." She'd still held out hope that he would remember. That she would come home to visit her parents, and magically he'd know her and declare his undying love. "A little while after that, I saw a picture of them together on Instagram, and I knew that I needed to let him go." She sighed. "So, I did."

Scar was quiet, but only for a moment. Then she was wrapping her arms around Fanny, holding her tight, and saying, "I'm so sorry, babe. I'm so, so sorry."

She smiled, shook her head. "It was a shitty situation, but I'm fine—"

"No." Scar pulled back, gripping the tops of her arms, and she was going to wrinkle her dress if she kept that up. "Don't you dare minimize what happened to you, to *both* of you. Yes, it was shitty. Yes, neither of you could control it. No, you don't get to tuck your pain away into some deep, dark hole inside you while putting on a mask, pretending to be okay. You don't have to pretend with me. You don't have to be okay."

Fanny's heart thudded, her eyes burned like a motherfucker.

Scarlett was . . . well, she was right.

And incredible. There was that, too.

"You're going to make me cry for real if you keep being so wonderful."

"Don't worry, it won't last."

That had Fanny snorting out a laugh, albeit a watery one. "Come on," she said, linking her arm with her friend's. "Let's go spend some money."

———

"You should give him a chance," Scar said a little while later, as they walked through the selection of shoes again. They'd already each found a pair and then had moved onto lingerie. Now they'd been ensnared by all the pretties again, and Fanny had been contemplating the need for another pair of strappy sandals.

For the record, she was well aware that she didn't need the sandals.

Want, on the other hand?

The want was real.

Fanny's feet slid to a stop, and she gaped up at Scarlett. After all she'd told her friend, Scar was just going to throw that out there like that? It wasn't for casual conversation, especially now that she knew the history. Plus, they'd been talking about going to

Molly's after this, and friends didn't throw friends curveballs when it came to drooling over or consuming carbs.

It was as simple as that.

"You know why I can't," she said.

"I know why you *haven't*," Scar countered.

"Plus, I don't even feel that way about him anymore," Fanny counter-countered, knowing it was a lie, but sticking by it anyway. Sometimes a girl had to lie to herself, and that was okay in her book.

But not, apparently, in *Scarlett's* book.

Her friend tossed her red locks over her shoulders, fixed Fanny with a look, and declared, "Bullshit."

"Hey, that's not—"

Scar held her in place with a piercing blue stare.

Fanny narrowed her eyes right back. "You've spent both interactions with him either telling him off, glaring at him, or staring at him longingly, with your face having gone soft." She said the last like it was a direct quote.

And it probably was.

Fucking Dani, spilling everything. "Yeah, so?"

"So?" Fanny asked incredulously. "So, you're supposed to be on my side. He's the bad guy in this—"

Scar lifted a brow. "To which I would have to say, that's more bullshit." A beat. "Also, which you know."

Okay, that *was* bullshit.

Scar smiled, probably knowing she'd won. The bitch.

She glared. If only Fanny didn't love her so much, she'd . . . do *something*.

Scarlett ran a finger over a pump. "Plus, I can't be the only one to get all the orgasms. He's hot, Fan. Those chocolate eyes—a woman could get lost in eyes like that. And not to mention the curls. Hell, I'm going on a date and spent the last couple of days thinking he was evil incarnate until Dani dished, but that still didn't stop me from imagining plunging my fingers into those curls and holding on tight while he—"

Fanny groaned, let her head fall back, not about to admit to all the times *she'd* lost herself in Brandon's eyes, nor how soft his curls had been against her bare skin, or how easy it had been to grip them when he'd positioned himself between her thighs.

He was probably even better than Scar could imagine.

And she'd bet her friend could imagine a lot.

And all her touching and getting lost in Brandon's eyes had been when she was barely an adult, both of them barely out of their teen years. He'd been all gangly muscles and still growing into himself. Nothing like what he was like now—the lines of his jaw fiercely defined and coated in a few days' worth of stubble, pecs she could grab on to, biceps that stretched the sleeves of his shirt, thighs and an ass that competed with the guys' on the Gold, and everyone knew that professional hockey players had the *best* thighs and asses. He was leaner than the guys but still fucking yummy.

This was a dangerous line of thinking, she knew, as her gaze moved to the fluorescent lights on the ceiling, and she sucked in a breath.

"He's hot, and you know it."

Her gaze flew down, met Scarlett's, and Fanny found herself cracking up when her friend waggled her brows and mimed something obscene and definitely not department store appropriate.

This conversation should hurt, especially after everything she'd told Scar, but instead, Fanny felt lighter, as though it were finally okay to have a normal conversation about Brandon. To be attracted to all his pretty, yummy muscles. To maybe even joke about him, or if not joke, then to at least withstand a little bit of teasing when it came to him and their interactions. It was that lightness that prompted her to say, "Oh, God, here we go. You didn't even like him two days ago."

"I have faith that he'll table the asshole."

Fanny snorted. "Because Dani bullied him into it?"

"No. Because Dani says he looks at you right."

Her lungs froze on a sharp inhale.

"Plus, he's not what I thought, and you know why," Scar went on, snagging her arm and jostling her slightly as she dragged her away from the pair of sandals Fanny definitely didn't need. "This would be different if you were over him or if it was obvious that you didn't feel anything for him or if he didn't look at you like you hung the moon and the sun and all the stars in the sky."

Fanny sucked in more air, liking that last part far too much for her mental well-being.

Scar squeezed her arm. "I'm not trying to push—"

"You're not?" Fanny said dryly.

"No." A shrug. "Well, okay, yes, I am." Scarlett grinned. "Because I can see on your face, your feelings are still there. You're not over him, even if you want to be, and I think . . ." She trailed off, nibbled on the corner of her mouth.

"What?" Fanny found herself asking.

"I think you're still in love with him."

Fanny stumbled back a step, shaking her head. "No, that's not—"

"Shit." Scar squeezed her arm again, drawing her to another table of shoes. "Just forget I said that. You're not ready and—"

Panic gripped Fanny, and she whipped around, picking up a random heel. "Look at this one. It'll be perfect with a dress, and you can even wear them with jeans or a—"

"Fanny."

"Or slacks. You could wear them with slacks!"

"*Fanny.*"

The sharp tone had her freezing, the heel in her hand.

"Ignore me," Scarlett murmured. "You're not ready."

Fat lot of good that did her with the words already swirling around her mind. Her emotions churned through her—the past and the memories and the growing glimmer of hope that was pushing her to track down Brandon, to tease out all the rest of her feelings, to take a step that would have her plummeting over the edge for him a third time.

Part of her wanted him. Part of her would *always* want him. Fuck.

"Fanny."

She glanced up at Scar, her pulse pounding in her veins, her throat tight and dry and—

"It'll be okay."

"I'm not so sure."

"Trust me." A beat. "And then ignore me."

Fanny shook her head. "Am I supposed to do both at the same time?"

"I believe I gave you an order for how to execute those two things already."

She glared, but at least her heart was slowing down, and she didn't feel at risk of passing out—at least for the moment.

"See?" Scarlett said, her lips turning up. "You're doing it already."

"What? The trusting or the ignoring?"

"Either." A grin. "Both." She plucked the heel Fanny didn't even realize she was still holding out of Fanny's hand and declared, "I like these. Let's both try them on."

Fanny swallowed hard, released a shaking breath, whispered, "I don't think I can."

"The shoes or Brandon?" Scar asked gently.

Fanny just looked at her.

Scar smiled kindly, nudged Fanny's shoulder with her own. "You don't have to decide today."

It felt that way, felt like Fanny needed to drop everything and figure out what to do with Brandon. But Scarlett was right. It was too much too soon, and she wasn't ready. "I—" she began, wanting to say something touching or emotional, or to at least express how much Scarlett's understanding meant to her.

But the words wouldn't come.

Luckily for Fanny, Scar heard them anyway.

"I know," she whispered. Then her chin came up, her volume

increased, and she said, "Now, let's go ask the salesperson for our sizes. We both absolutely *need* these shoes."

————

She'd put away her new shoes—two pairs, the heels she and Scarlett had both tried on *and* the strappy sandals that she hadn't been able to get out of her head.

Funny how that kept going around, huh?

But she wasn't thinking about that, nor about Brandon or the notebook that was sitting on the kitchen island, burning a hole in the granite (figuratively, not literally, otherwise she would have much bigger problems in her life than an ex-fiancé with a memory problem).

And look.

She was joking in her own mind.

That was good, right?

That had to mean she was right to talk to Scarlett about Brandon and everything that went down, rather than continue to bottle it all up and pretend it hadn't happened. It was on the surface and exposed and—

Why that notebook was burning the proverbial hole.

Because she'd put away her purchases, had whipped up dinner —salad and leftover soup from Molly's, which Scarlett had treated her to after they spent their wad on shoes and lace (for *her*, not for Brandon, Fanny promised herself). Then she'd gone the whole popcorn, movie, wine route.

But that hadn't held her attention.

Every time she moved into the kitchen to refill her glass or get more popcorn or . . . hell, who was she kidding?

She kept going into the kitchen because she wanted to look in the damned notebook. It was time she admitted that and stopped lying to herself and . . . she wanted to know what Brandon's mom had intended her to have.

There. That was the truth.

No amount of fake blood and suspenseful music would change the truth.

She'd already torn open those barely scabbed-over wounds, had already told Scar everything, and plus, she'd forgiven Brandon long ago, was now nurturing the spark inside her that kept telling her to move forward.

And . . .

No more excuses.

She put down the wine glass, left the movie running in the background because the sound of the film was oddly comforting, and she moved to the island.

Releasing a shuddering breath, Fanny flipped open the cover.

The picture pasted to the inside had her breath shuddering all over again. It was of her and Brandon, both looking so damned young. He was in his hockey gear. She was in her skating leotard, earmuffs covering her ears, the fingertips of her gloves damp. Their arms were around each other. Their smiles huge.

God, she'd never stood a chance without him, had she?

He'd owned her heart, been that missing piece she hadn't even known she was lacking from the first moment he'd teased her when they were teenagers.

Sighing, she turned the page and began reading what appeared to be Grace's journal, or maybe it was more of a memory book. The entries were sporadic and only mentioned Brandon and his activities, and as she read about Brandon's hockey tournaments, the paper he got an A on in school, a memory sparked across Fanny's mind. She remembered seeing Grace writing in this, and her breath caught as she realized what the entries began to include.

Her.

Fanny was in these.

Grace had written about Brandon being infatuated with a girl. Then the first time she met Fanny and how much she had liked her.

Fan let her fingers drift across the words, wonder sliding through her. Grace had liked her.

Really liked her.

Okay, she'd known that, had felt that affection and love over the years, but there was something about actually seeing it in words, seeing it in something private. These were Grace's inner thoughts, and there wasn't any veneer of politeness.

And Grace had liked Fanny.

So that was big, and it had Fanny continuing to read, devouring the entries, the story of her and Brandon through Grace's eyes, and by the time she reached the end, she didn't know what to think.

Or maybe it was that she knew what to think, what she should be doing.

Who she should be running to.

But what she was too terrified to do.

"Fuck," she whispered as she read the last entry, the sadness Grace felt when Fanny had left for good.

I feel like I've lost a daughter. I'm so happy to have Brandon healthy and whole, happy that he's found someone to love . . . I just wish that someone could have been Fanny.

She closed the cover and stood, her heart pounding, her eyes stinging.

It was too much, too raw, too real.

Too close, when she'd spent so long trying to create distance between her past and present. Too open and out there when she'd worked so hard to rivet the lid on her past.

She turned for the front door without thinking, scooping up her keys, her skate bag.

She hurried outside, not caring that it was late and dark, and the rink would be closed.

Unlock her car. Her bag in the passenger's seat.

Her keys in the ignition.

Go.

Run.

Find a way to shove it all down again.

EIGHT

BRANDON

He pulled up to Fanny's house, still intending to just drive by.

Or maybe to pause at the curb and try to figure out how to make things right between them.

Or maybe to park next to her car and pretend he had a right to be there.

Or maybe—

To see Fanny run right out the front door and hightail it for her car. She didn't look around. She didn't notice his car at the curb. She didn't seem to notice anything as she all but ran down the walkway and tossed a bag into her passenger's seat and tore off out of the driveway.

As though the hounds of hell were chasing her.

It wasn't even a decision to follow her.

She drove away, and he immediately trailed her, his mind spinning, worry swirling through him. What had happened? Was she okay? Hurt?

His jaw was tight, fingers clenched on the steering wheel.

He was going to find out.

Her car hovered above the speed limit on the freeway for the couple of exits they were on it then did the same as she drove through the quiet streets, as she whipped into a familiar parking lot.

She stopped by the curb, and he watched as she got out, bag in hand, and unlocked the glass and steel doors, disappearing inside the darkened ice rink. Her skates must be in that bag, he knew now. Just as Brandon understood why she'd run out of her house, why she'd come here.

Fanny needed to out-skate her demons.

Which meant he should leave.

He knew he was going to stay anyway.

He parked behind her car, promising that he'd wait out here until she was done, would make sure she made it home safe.

He made it all of ten minutes before he got out of his car.

Fanny hadn't locked the door behind her.

He quietly slipped inside, making sure the glass and metal panel shut behind him, allowing his eyes to adjust to the dim lobby.

There were a few lights on in the rinks beyond—four in total—but he moved straight ahead, going to the sheet of ice he'd seen Fanny on both times he'd been here before. There was barely enough illumination to see the edges of the ice, the plastic boards surrounding it, topped by clear plexiglass.

And there certainly wasn't enough light to expose him where he stood just inside the second set of doors, shadows clinging to the walls, the bleachers filling up one side of the space.

But apparently, it was enough for Fanny to see, to do what she needed to do.

Her bag sat on the floor, open in front of that lowest bench of the bleachers, almost spotlit beneath one of the few lights that were on.

But that only drew his focus for a couple of seconds.

Because his eyes . . . they were drawn to the ice. To *Fanny* on the ice.

God, she still moved like a river, liquid and smooth and persistent. No barrier would stop her, but it wasn't brutal like a tidal wave, like the ocean swallowing up the coastline. She was the narrow stretch of a creek, flowing through rocks and trees, along the riverbed. Graceful and effortless and absolutely stunning.

There wasn't any music blaring over the speakers. There weren't any fans in the stands.

It was just her and the music in her heart, the joy in her soul.

He stood there, riveted in place, the only sound in the large space the crunch of her skate blades against the ice. She owned the rink, using every inch as she moved through a stretch of footwork he remembered her taking months to master. Only it was different at the end, as though she'd added to it and increased the difficulty of the movements. Then she picked up speed, skating around the edges, lining up for a takeoff. There was one less rotation than he'd seen the last time she'd performed, but the double axel was still impressive, as was the Lutz she entered into barely a heartbeat later.

But she didn't stop there.

She continued moving, flowing, and it was as though a decade had never passed.

She jumped again and again. Her skate blades glinted in the dim light.

Her chest heaved, and her hair was plastered to her forehead.

And then . . .

She stopped, her gaze arrowing toward him.

NINE

FANNY

She was in the middle of her routine, the one that had earned her a silver medal.

The one she'd tweaked and added to over the years. Taking out some of the more difficult jumps—because she wasn't in as good of shape as she'd been at seventeen and didn't like breaking her ass—but putting in some of the footwork she really enjoyed. That had become her specialty, mainly because she'd needed to be good enough to teach other people how to trust their edges, their balance, to correctly distribute their weight.

She'd spent hours and hours upping her game.

And tonight just flowed.

All of the tension and need and longing that had coalesced upon finishing reading that notebook flowed out of her as she skated to music she hadn't heard in more than a decade.

The last time she'd skated it with music, she'd been surrounded by thousands of people. Her parents had come, along with Brandon's, and they'd all been sitting together in the stands. But she'd only had eyes for him. For the boy she loved. The boy who knew every move in the program and would mouth them as she completed them.

Something she'd only discovered when a reporter had shown her video of Brandon doing it in the stands.

So fucking good.

He'd been so fucking good.

Was it any wonder that no one else had ever competed? How could they?

She'd had the perfect man, the perfect boyfriend and fiancé and . . . lost it.

Tears prickled at the edges of her eyes, but only for a second, because rage quickly followed, chasing them away. Rage at what she'd lost. Rage at herself for being scared of what might be between them now. Rage at Brandon for getting sick, for forgetting her even though she knew logically it wasn't his fault.

But logic wasn't ruling her right now.

The fury of the last ten years was.

She moved faster and faster, speeding through the footwork, then picking up speed as she circled the rink, prepping for a jump, a toe loop that was messy as hell because she was sucking wind, but she pushed on anyway, forcing herself into another double axel with her chest heaving.

She stumbled, hit the ice with one knee, her hands catching herself on the ice.

Dropping her head as she tried to control her breathing, she stayed in place, her one knee aching from the impact, her fingers burning as the cold soaked into her skin, her palms.

Her nape prickled, and her gaze jerked up.

She shouldn't be able to see him, not with the shadows, not with the dim light.

But some part of her knew he was there. *How* was he there?

He just was, moving out of the darkness, stepping toward the door of the rink, the loud metal *thunk* echoing through the quiet of the space as he opened it. As he waited.

And she couldn't stop herself from going through their old

routine, the movements as natural as breathing. She pushed to her feet and skated to that open door, stopping in it, her chest still heaving, her fingers gripping the cold plastic of the boards.

Beautiful.

The man was so fucking beautiful. She wanted to stroke the stubble on his cheeks and jaw. She was desperate to see if he tasted the same. She wanted his strong arms to band around her. She wanted him to declare that he loved her and wanted her forever, even though Fanny knew that would terrify her.

So she stayed there, fingers aching from denying herself the need to touch.

His voice was barely above a whisper, his soft question familiar and part of that old routine. "Are you done?" And when she found herself shaking her head, Brandon just brushed his knuckles over her cheek then nudged her back slightly.

She turned.

The door closed.

And she went back to skating, starting that routine from the beginning, throwing every bit of skill she possessed into her movements, those long minutes of her, the ice, and Brandon. For herself, because she never felt freer than when she was skating, when she was pushing herself to the limit on the cold, hard surface, when she was moving in a way that spoke to her soul.

Only when her legs felt like they were going to fall off did she glance back up, half-expecting Brandon to be gone. But he was still standing there on the other side of the door, his gaze on her, his body statue still.

He opened the door when she came over again, not asking this time if she was done, only taking her hand when she stepped down onto the black mat that surrounded the rink, and like he used to, he nudged her to her skate bag sitting by the bottom row of the bleachers. Brandon knelt before her then undid her skates, and it was falling into another memory as he carefully dried the blades and covered them with her skate guards before putting them into her bag.

A moment later, he helped her slip her feet into her fuzzy boots before picking up her skate bag and then taking her hand again.

His fingers were warm and rough as they held on to hers, and they walked out of the rink together, the past and the present all twisted together as she locked up, before he walked her to her car.

They stopped, and her heart pounded as she stared up into his pretty face, wanting . . .

Too much.

Everything.

Nothing.

"You're beautiful," he murmured, releasing her hand to cup her cheek, and she couldn't stop herself from leaning into his palm, couldn't stop those words from soaking into her skin, her heart. "And you still move like liquid silk."

Her lips parted, and she rose on tiptoe, needing to be closer, desperate to taste him. "I read the notebook."

His eyes widened. "Yeah?"

She nodded. "Yeah."

"What did you think?" he asked gently.

What *did* she think? Too much, that was what. That was why she'd fled the quiet of her house, the tangled feelings pressing in on her. "I . . ."

His head dropped, his hot, damp breath on her skin.

"Fanny," he whispered.

She shuddered, leaned closer, pleasure coursing through her when her breasts brushed against his chest. "I think we had a lot of good times," she murmured, her hand resting on his shoulder.

He ran his knuckles over her cheek. "I think we could have a lot more."

Inhaling, the air thickened, and time disappeared. It was just her and Brandon and the moonlight, the whisper of the breeze, the deep longing to go back to what they had before, to forget everything and just . . . touch her lips to his.

Closer, he moved.

Nearer, she leaned.

His mouth was right there. He smelled of mint and spice, of sandalwood and something musky that made her want to rub herself against him.

His breath mingled with hers. His hand slid down, cupped the side of her neck, and . . . he kissed her forehead.

Then. Stepped. Back.

Fanny's nostrils flared on a sharp inhale, but before she could say anything, before she could close the distance between them and get the kiss she wanted, he snagged her keys from her hand, unlocked her car, and guided her into the driver's seat. Head spinning from the sudden change of circumstances—from his arms to her car—she couldn't summon any words when he bent over her and set her bag on the passenger's seat, pausing only to buckle her seat belt before he straightened and stood.

"Drive safe, honey," he whispered.

He shut the door.

She blinked, hands finding the steering wheel and clenching the leather-covered circle tightly. Need was coiled tight in her stomach, damp heat had gathered between her thighs. She wanted him, wanted to open her door and go to him. To kiss him.

She fumbled for the handle, started to open the door.

Lights flared to life behind her.

Eyes flying to the rearview, she saw his silhouette, saw him sitting in his car, watched as he pulled away from the curb.

Her hand relaxed, dropping away from the handle, and no, that wasn't disappointment coursing through her. It wasn't. She glanced down and saw that her keys were in the cupholder; she picked them up with shaking fingers. A deep breath steadied her, tempered her need, her disappointment she was pretending wasn't disappointment still sitting heavy in her gut.

"Okay," she said on a long, slow sigh.

She turned on her car and drove away from the rink.

But that disappointment that wasn't disappointment faded when she noticed the headlights in her rearview again, when she watched Brandon's car pull behind her again, when he followed her all the way home.

When those headlights didn't disappear into the night until she was safe in her house.

Then there was no more disappointment, pretend or otherwise.

There was only the small kernel of hope.

———

By the next night, after not enough sleep, too many hours of clinics, and not one glimpse or call or text or barging onto her front porch of Brandon, that kernel of hope was very much at risk of disappearing.

She hadn't expected him to show at the rink.

For one, he didn't know her schedule, wouldn't know if she'd be teaching or not.

For another, the man had a job, and it wasn't like he could just drop everything to come seek her out.

But still, he hadn't texted, and he hadn't shown, and now it was ten at night and . . . nothing. Not one word or call or text. And yes, she was cognizant of the fact that he didn't have her number. But part of her wanted the man to work for it—or to keep working for it, anyway.

That he didn't?

That he didn't ring her doorbell during dinner or after it, even though she'd lingered downstairs for much longer than normal, pretending to watch a movie while really staring out the window, searching for any glimpse of a car pulling up to her house, threatened to extinguish that tiny flame of hope.

She tried for logic—it hadn't even been twenty-four hours, he didn't have her number, they were both up late the night before, amongst others—but it wasn't particularly successful.

And then her phone buzzed.

And the way her heart pounded as she reached for it was a

damned good indication of how deep she was already in with him, despite her fighting the slide every inch of the way.

Her eyes flicked over the message, barely reading the words before she realized that it wasn't from Brandon.

Acute disappointment swept through her.

Strong enough that she dropped her phone on the bed and pushed out from beneath the covers, pacing to her window and staring out at the back yard, trying desperately to calm herself, to push down the feelings that threatened to overwhelm.

When she could breathe without it hurting, Fanny turned back to her phone and opened up the text.

Hi, Fanny. This is Charlie. I hope it's okay to text. Scarlett gave me your number.

So much for Scar thinking she was in—lalala—love with Brandon, or thinking Fan should give him another chance. Here she was, throwing her at her brother. She typed out a text to her friend.

You gave your brother my number?

A few minutes passed before her cell vibrated.

He's a good guy. Give him a chance.

"Give *who* a chance?" she muttered. "Brandon or Charlie?" Sighing, she tossed her phone down in disgust and paced away to the window again, staring out like the shadows might give her some answers . . . or like Brandon might appear out of them again, might watch her and hold her hand and this time, might kiss her somewhere that *wasn't* her forehead.

Her phone buzzed.

She couldn't stop herself from going over and reading the message.

Now I'm thinking I overstepped. Sorry about that. If you feel up to hanging out, hit me up sometime.

Damn.

Why did Charlie have to seem nice?

Why hadn't Brandon come over?

The second more than the first—and maybe later she would need to look into herself to truly understand her motivations and whether texting Charlie back and asking if he wanted to go to dinner the next night when she was so torn up with Brandon made her a giant asshole or not.

She was pretty certain it did.

But either way, she sent the message.

And when Charlie called her back instead of texting, she picked up the call. She talked and flirted and got to know him for almost an hour. Scar was right. He *was* nice. And funny. And he had a nice voice.

And none of the complications of Brandon.

So when she yawned as it neared midnight, and he apologized for keeping her up so late then asked if she really did want to grab dinner, she accepted the invitation. She even went so far as to suggest a place to meet since he was new to town.

She was going to give him a chance.

Charlie.

Not Brandon.

TEN

BRANDON

"I'm married, and my wife wants me to take another woman on a date," Devon snapped (again, since he didn't appear to be anywhere near ready to let it go) as he stormed into the conference room, bypassing the empty chair at the table and stomping to the coffee pot. As he poured himself a mug, Olivia glanced up from her phone and rolled her eyes.

Brandon smothered a smile.

It had been two days since he'd last seen Fanny. Well, fine. Technically it had only been one, if he counted that he'd trailed her home well past midnight the previous day. Not seeing her yesterday was hard as hell, but they'd made some progress at the rink, and he didn't want to push her too far.

I think we had a lot of good times.

She hadn't discounted what they had. Instead, she'd softened in his hold, had allowed him to touch her, to take care of her in one small way.

Progress.

But he knew he needed to play this carefully.

So, he hadn't gone over to her house last night, and he hadn't called her, even though he'd managed to get her number via Kaydon, who'd gotten it from someone in the Gold organization (which equaled Brandon being on the radar of the Gold and their gossiping hockey players, not that he cared). He'd gotten an in with Fanny, and he was going to do this slow and smart and steady. He would convince her to give him a chance, and he wasn't going to fuck it up by playing the bull in a china shop.

"A date!" Devon said again.

Olivia sighed. "I thought we were beyond this."

Devon scowled and stomped over, dropping into his chair and pouting. "I am. I'm doing it, even though I hate it." He sipped, plunked the mug onto the table.

"For the children," Olivia said, lips twitching, tone dry.

Dev narrowed his eyes. "Yes," he gritted. "I'm doing it for the children."

Olivia glanced at Brandon, which was really shit timing on his part because he was trying to hold it together, and seeing her blue eyes sparkling with mirth had him losing any hope of control. He burst out laughing, and Olivia joined in.

Devon glared at them. "You're both assholes."

"You love us," Olivia said, wiping her eyes. "You know it's true."

"I tolerate you."

"Love." She pushed out of her chair, pressed a kiss to his cheek, and swiped his coffee, sucking down a long sip. "As in, you love us both because we bring you excellent clients and negotiate kickass contracts."

"I hates you."

"Hates?" Brandon couldn't help but say.

Olivia started laughing again as she refilled his mug and plunked it back in front of Devon. "What, are you Gollum?"

Devon growled. "It's my precious," he muttered, snatching the mug.

"Which? The coffee or Becca?" Brandon asked.

Dev pointed a finger at him. "I don't like that you feel comfortable enough to give me shit already."

Brandon chuckled. "Bet you're kicking yourself for giving me that signing bonus, too."

"Fuck yeah, I am," Dev muttered. "But now I'm looking for a reason to fire you."

"And here I was going to offer to take your place," Brandon said. "If you could sell the organizers on Dinner with a Sports Agent instead of Dinner with the Sexiest Man of the Year."

"It was the Month. One *fucking* month, one *fucking* time."

"Your life is so tough," Olivia crooned. "Being a sexy hockey player." She pretended to swoon, the back of her hand going to her forehead. "Oh, the humanity."

Dev sighed. "I hates."

Olivia grinned. "I know."

Then Dev turned to Brandon. "You'd seriously do that?"

"After hearing you moan over this date for the past few days?" Brandon asked dryly. "Fuck, yes. Hell, I consider it a public service."

He glanced at Olivia. "Think you can convince my wife to make the switch?"

A smirk curved her lush mouth. "What'll you give me?"

Dev widened his eyes. "My undying love?"

"Pft." She waved a hand and leaned back in her chair, and Brandon could only smile as he watched her put her negotiating hat on. There was a reason she was at Prestige, and that was because she was damned good at squeezing perks out of contracts for her clients. "I'm thinking a trip to Aruba."

Dev snorted. "Like you'll get Cole off that farm of his."

One black brow lifted. "Who said I want him to go with me?"

Touché, Brandon thought, watching the two of them go back and forth as he smothered a smile.

"Two weeks at the resort you took Becca to."

Dev glared. "You trying to bankrupt me?"

A roll of her eyes. "If one trip would bankrupt you, we have bigger problems to discuss."

"Olivia," Dev warned.

She studied her nails. "Either that or you can talk to Bex yourself."

Dev was silent for a long moment. "No trip. What else?"

"Jewels."

He sniffed, shook his head. "Dude."

"I'm not a dude," she said sweetly. "Okay then, no trip, no jewels. My price is a new pair of heels."

Dev made a noise of outrage. "Those would be more expensive than a trip to fucking Aruba."

A shrug. "Do I need to remind you that you are in the position of disadvantage in this negotiation?"

"Baked goods?" Dev countered without acknowledging that true statement. He wouldn't give the point any credence because it would give Olivia even more power. And but seriously, Brandon felt as though he were attending a master class in negotiating.

"Ah, once that would have been golden," she said. "But alas for you, Cole gets Molly's to cater the ranch." A silken smile curving her fire engine red mouth as she waved a hand with all the regal demeanor of a queen. "But by all means, however, keep trying."

Devon's phone buzzed, and he muttered a curse. "Logan is here to sign the contract." He glared at Olivia. "Fine. Heels. Your choice. But only if you convince Becca to allow Brandon to take my place."

Olivia sighed as she slicked on a fresh layer of lipstick, even though the crimson color had looked perfect before she'd put on the newest coat, at least from what Brandon could tell. "It's not going to be easy."

Brandon could practically hear the bones of Devon's jaw clenching together. "Fine. *Two* pairs."

She smacked her lips together. "Three."

A vein pulsed in Dev's forehead before he nodded. "Three."

There was a knock at the door, and Olivia got up to answer it. On the way, she stopped and pressed a kiss to Dev's cheek, wiping off the red mark she'd left behind before moving to the door. "One pair," she said, smiling widely. "I can't help myself with negotiating, but I'm not going to drain my godchildren's college funds."

The tension left Devon's frame.

Brandon bit back another laugh.

Olivia opened the door and let Logan in.

And yeah, Brandon had just been lucky enough to witness that master class in negotiation.

Olivia was the shit.

———

He sipped the beer and wondered how quickly he could get out of there.

Not that he didn't like Ethan, Kaydon, and Logan. He did. The latter two were talented players and good guys, and Kay and he were close. But he especially liked Ethan after Brandon had apologized for the other night and explained in the most general terms possible what was going on with him and Fanny. Ethan had nodded his understanding then promised to disembowel him if he ever talked to Fanny like that again.

Brandon hadn't protested.

Mainly because if he did talk to her like that again, then he'd deserve the disemboweling.

But he liked that Fanny had people in her corner who'd protect her.

He liked that Ethan wouldn't stand in his way.

Because he'd decided to win her over. He wasn't desperate to try to earn forgiveness—he was lucky enough to have that—now he was going to weave his way back into Fanny's life and prove to her that he was worth whatever risk the future might bring.

Luckily, Ethan hadn't held a grudge—aside from the whole disemboweling threats—especially after Brandon had bought the first two rounds.

He was itching to get over to Fanny's, but he knew this time was important.

Not just to build the relationship with Kaydon as a client, but also because if he was going to build a full life with Fanny, that meant *he* needed to have a full life. He needed friends, and it wouldn't hurt if one of those friends happened to be the significant other of one of *her* friends. Maybe that was an Olivia-level move, but either way, he liked Ethan, would be happy to be friends with him.

Ethan's relationship with Fanny was just a side benefit.

Logan was a good guy, too. He'd been in the league for many years and had a whole wealth of interesting stories to go with it. He'd also been cool about taking Kaydon under his wing, having been through a similar injury early in his own career.

And fuck, did Brandon hate that Kaydon hadn't discussed the toxic environment at his last team with him.

Kay was a head-down-move-forward kind of guy, and though his work ethic had never faded, and he'd fought to push through the injury, though he did his level best to prove his mettle to the management at the to-remain-nameless team, none of those factors could fix a shitty work environment.

He'd been lucky to be released and luckier to be picked up by the Gold.

And not with a low-ball, insulting offer that he'd been given by other teams. With a fair bottom line and potential for growth if he really started rolling in the league.

Brandon had a feeling about this season.

He felt in his bones that the timing was right, and Kay had the right crew behind him, the right players with him. He knew, just *knew*, this would be Kaydon's year.

"So then Brit took off," Logan said. "But we were ready. Blane tackled her and stole her shoes, thinking that would slow her down."

Brandon grinned.

Kay leaned forward. "Did it?"

"No," Ethan said, shaking his head with a bemused smile. "She just ran barefoot and beat all of us anyway."

"And then we got in trouble from Mandy because Brit got a cut on the bottom of her foot."

Brandon started laughing. "The women stick together."

"The women," Logan said dryly, "like to stick it to us."

Ethan shrugged. "It's true."

"So, that's why you guys have given up . . ." Kaydon started asking, but Brandon stopped listening. Because the door to the bar had opened and a good-looking blond man had walked in.

Though that wasn't what had caught Brandon's focus.

No, every cell in his body shot to rigid attention at the woman walking in behind him. A brunette with curves he would know anywhere, with lips he needed to kiss, with eyes that were stunning, with a heart he needed to own.

He almost jumped off his stool, almost left the high-top table they'd occupied since coming to the brewery an hour before, but Kay laughed loudly at something, and that broke through the red haze coating his vision enough to think.

Think, Cunningham, he snapped to himself.

Maybe it was a business meeting.

They could totally just be here to discuss something with her business. He'd been researching it since the first time he'd seen her at the rink, knew it was growing, and there were quite a few organizations interested in partnering with her.

The door shut, and Fanny laughed as she trailed the blond man to the hostess stand.

Definitely a business meeting. Def—

They checked in and stepped to the side, probably waiting for their table, and the man slipped a hand around her waist as she leaned into him.

She let him touch her.
She. Let. Him. Touch. Her.
Touch. *Her*.
Not a business meeting. Not a *fucking* business meeting.
She was on a date.
Fuck *that*.

ELEVEN

FANNY

Charlie was great.

Good-looking. Funny. Attentive and sweet.

But . . . she didn't feel a modicum of attraction toward him. He was all those things she'd mentioned, but she didn't want to jump his bones. Hell, she'd take a slight urge to cuddle at this point.

Instead, every time he touched her, a light hand on her back, guiding her through a door, their fingers brushing when he pulled back her chair for her, she could only think of how it had felt when Brandon had touched her outside the rink. Or when his hand had pressed to her stomach, keeping her from stepping onto the glass on her porch that night.

Or his palm on her cheek.

Or—

"You okay?" Charlie asked.

She blinked, shook her head slightly. "Sorry, I zoned out there for a minute."

"I knew I shouldn't have started discussing the atomic weight of sodium hydroxide." He made a face, though he couldn't hold it, his lips turning up at the edges, eyes dancing with humor, letting her know that he hadn't been testing her on her chemistry skills. "Told you I was out of practice with the whole dating scene." He tapped a finger to his mouth. "I know what will keep you riveted," he teased. "I can tell you all about my success on my track and field team in high school."

Laughter bubbled up in her chest as she reached over and squeezed his hand. "I'd be happy to hear of your accolades," she said. "Was it long jump?"

He flipped his hand over, lacing their fingers together.

They were warm and calloused and . . . nothing like Brandon's.

Fuck.

"Not long jump. I was a hundred meter guy," he said. "But I'm not the one who has a silver medal. What was *that* like?" he asked.

See? He was good.

Sharing about himself, but then able to return the favor, to encourage *her* to share. This man wouldn't stay single for long. She should jump in, grab on, and—

He wasn't Brandon.

"It's okay if you don't want to talk about it," he said, squeezing her fingers. "I'm sure you get sick of discussing it."

"No," she said, forcing herself to focus. It wasn't fair to Charlie. "It's hard to put into words." Her eyes slid closed, and she felt her mouth curve, able to transport herself right back to that moment. "I didn't fully achieve my goal of gold, but it still felt incredible to be on that podium. I remember the weight of the medal. I remember seeing my boy—" She stopped herself before she could say boyfriend or mentioned Brandon. "I remember seeing my *family*"—her true family, Jeff and Grace, even though they sat next to her biological parents—"in the stands, and the smiles they wore, how proud they looked. I remember seeing the flag being hoisted, the sound of the crowd and the music blaring through the arena. Russia's anthem." She opened her eyes and grinned at him. "It wasn't the Star-Spangled Banner, though it *was* still captivating."

Charlie squeezed her fingers.

And she found herself still talking, even though he'd been right, and she didn't like to talk about it. Even without the gold medal, she was proud of herself, proud of the work she'd put in. It was just . . . everything else that had come after had turned those memories into something that she buried rather than relished. She sighed. "But looking back now, it was like everything during that time was on fast-forward. Before the medal ceremony, everything was almost a blur with all the training and press and ice time and then competing. After, it was closing ceremonies—we were right near the end, and I didn't have much time to do anything besides focus on the competition—and more press and finally getting some sleep. So, when I was finally done and could actually let loose a bit, it was over."

"A whirlwind," Charlie said.

Her lips curved. "Precisely."

"Your parents must have been so proud of you," he said.

Ah. Well, that was almost as complicated of a topic as Brandon.

Both of which were way too complicated to get into a discussion about on a first date.

Which was why she simply said, "Yes."

Seeming to understand that was a touchy subject, he straightened slightly, still holding her hand. "Dessert? Or should I take you home so you can get some sleep?"

Her heart squeezed, and she knew—freaking *knew*—that if she weren't hung up on an annoying, curly-haired, handsome ex-fiancé, that he would be really good for her. He probably would be really good for her even with her still hung up on Brandon.

But he deserved someone without entanglements.

Someone better than her.

"Dessert," she said, wanting to pretend a little longer. "You pick." She tugged her hand back, started to push back her chair. "I need to use the bathroom."

"Is this a test?" Charlie asked lightly, standing when she did. Polite.

Probably *too* polite, considering who his sister was.

She shook her head. "How are you Scarlett's brother?"

"Why?" he asked, tucking a lock of hair behind her ear. "Because I have manners?"

"Precisely."

He grinned. "My mom taught us both. Scar ignored her."

"And you?"

His eyes, a deep blue, darkened enough to cause an answering echo in her middle, telling her that yeah, this man could be trouble, just like his sister. "I only put them to use for very special occasions."

Laughing and shaking her head, she stepped by him. "Order dessert, and if you pass, I might consider a second date."

Saluting, he sat back down and picked up the smaller dessert menu their server had left on the table not too long before. "Chocolate?" he asked, glancing up at her.

"Cheater."

"Or are you not a chocolate woman?"

Half her mouth turned up. "I'll never tell."

"Cheesecake?"

"Did you get in trouble in school for cheating?"

"No." A beat. "But only because I never got caught."

She giggled. Actually giggled. Then realized she was standing in the middle of the restaurant, blocking the walkway, and still not walking to the bathroom. Charlie was trouble all right. Just like his sister. Pointing a finger in his direction, she ordered, "Dessert."

And then she swept through the tables and into the hallway that led to the bathrooms.

Fanny was about to push into the single stall when a hand

caught her arm and dragged her back against a hard, warm chest. "Charlie!" she gasped.

The fingers tightened.

The spicy male scent reached her nose.

And she knew, even before he spoke.

"Not Charlie," Brandon growled. He spun her, pinned her to the wall, his body pressing to hers, and it was . . . glorious. Everything she'd imagined, *more*. Because it was familiar and not, and the feel of him against her had a swath of heat rolling through her, hardening her nipples, bringing her thighs together, squeezing tight against the sudden burst of moisture drenching her panties as she arched against him.

"Brandon," she whispered.

"What the fuck are you doing on a date with another man?" he snapped.

She lifted her chin, anger pulsing, twining with her desire in some sort of fucked-up need for this man. She pushed at his chest. "Go away."

"Why?" he asked hotly, not moving, not even when she put all her force behind her shoves.

"Fuck you," she hissed, raging now.

He leaned heavier against her, causing her breathing to hitch. "Why are you with that asshole?"

"I can date who I want," she gritted out. "You don't have any right to—"

"Why?" he repeated.

And something snapped inside her. "Because you didn't come. Because I waited all day for you to call and show up, but you didn't. And I wanted you to." She shoved him hard, forcing him back a step. "Damn you, I wanted you to. I wanted . . . *you*."

His eyes widened. "Fanny," he breathed.

She started to clamp a hand over her mouth, unable to believe she'd said that. She was on a date with another man right now, and Charlie was great, and she didn't want to go back to the past. They couldn't ever be what they once were.

Right? *Right?*

But even as he stepped closer, she didn't push him away, she didn't leave that hall.

Even as his mouth lowered to hers, she didn't retreat.

She stretched up, lifted her chin . . . aligned their lips.

And kissed him.

Or maybe he kissed her. Or maybe—

Fuck if she didn't really care.

He parted her lips with a dart of his tongue, slipping it into her mouth and coaxing hers out to play. Sleek darts and shallow teases. His fingers sliding up along her side, her arm, her neck, before slipping back and weaving into her hair, tilting her head, and angling them.

It was new . . . and not.

It was familiar . . . and not.

It was . . . Brandon.

She moaned and wrapped her arms around his neck, bringing him closer, wanting his body flush against her, needing him close after he'd been far for so long. His other hand cupped her ass, brought her leg up. Without a moment of hesitation, she wrapped it around his waist, and then the other. His groan when he pressed her against the wall, their bodies perfectly aligned, the hard length of his cock insistent against the fabric of her underwear had her shivering, uncaring that anyone might walk down the hall and see them.

His fingers massaged her ass, his hips moved, grinding against her, and she was shockingly close to an orgasm in a matter of seconds.

"Bran," she gasped, when he pulled away and nipped at her lips then bent to nip at her throat, the bared skin just above her breasts.

"So fucking beautiful," he whispered against her skin, tongue gliding along her flesh, along the seam of the deep V of her dress.

Down. Down. *Down.*

Until it felt like she'd fall, until it was only his hand and the pressure of his hips that kept her against that wall.

And then she wasn't thinking of falling.

Wasn't thinking of anything except the fact that his tongue was darting *in*. That it was slipping under the fabric of her dress and unerringly finding the hard tip of her nipple.

"No bra," he whispered, flicking his tongue there.

She moaned, and though a distant part of her understood this was insane, that she should push him away . . . the rest of her wanted Brandon too much to be thinking clearly.

She yanked the fabric to the side, and he didn't delay, just sucked her nipple deeply into his mouth and kept rocking against her. Sparks were shooting through her nerves, glittering pleasure was filling her veins, need and heat and moisture were gathering and coiling and . . .

Exploding.

Between her thighs, flooding the rest of body, a rapid surge that tightened every muscle and cell, one that flew through her with all the intensity of a lightning strike. And then it relaxed, her pleasure lapping at her, slowly receding, fading until it ebbed against her like gentle waves against a shore.

"Fuck, you're beautiful," he murmured, slowly tucking her back into her dress and kissing his way back up her throat until he reached her mouth.

He kissed her again, kissed her until she was reduced to ash, until she was reformed into someone completely different.

Only then did he slowly unhook her legs, placing her feet on the floor one by one, steadying her until she found her balance, his fingers and hold gentle now instead of whipping her into a frenzy of need.

"Beautiful," he said with another brush of his lips.

He straightened, stroked his thumb over her cheek.

"Get rid of him," he ordered.

And then he was gone.

Leaving her panting and alone in the hallway, wondering what in the fuck had just happened.

―――――

Kaydon looked toward the door to the rink, and she would have had to be blind to miss the longing in his eyes.

"All right," she muttered. "All right." She nodded to the exit. "Get out of here."

He didn't question her, just tossed out a wave and hauled ass to the door. "Thanks, Fanny," he called before taking off down the hall, "that was fun."

She grinned.

He didn't have to pretend it had been fun.

She knew it had been a combination of boring, small, repetitive movements he'd done a million times throughout the years and exhausting on-ice maneuvers that he'd never done before. He'd be sore tomorrow—and probably the night after—but it was the only way he would be able to properly relearn the muscle memory. At least to relearn it properly.

Because he'd had several seasons of skating through the pain.

Then another of jumping back onto the ice without proper rehab.

He had all sorts of shit to work through, and it was going to take some more time in order to get there.

Which was why she called, "See you next week!"

His groan echoed down the hallway.

She grinned, started to follow him, ready to get off the ice herself, but a voice called her name. Turning, she skated over to the little girl who'd been patiently waiting for the public skate to start. Opening the gate to let everyone on, she bent to hear the girl over the rush of kids jostling to get on. "Can I show you my axel?"

Fanny's heart squeezed. "I'd love to see it, Lily."

This was why she taught, and not just the big guys who thought puck handling was more important, but because it was a fucking joy to see skating through the eyes of kids. It was new and fresh and exciting. Especially in the littlest kids.

"Yay!" She snagged Fanny's hand and all but dragged her to the corner. "Stand here."

Fanny stood there.

Lily skated a few circles to warm up, then lined up her take-off, jumped, and . . . fell.

Closing the distance between them, she helped Lily up. "You were too far forward on your landing. Bend your knee a bit more to even out your weight, and that'll help for next time." She demonstrated. "Ready to try again?"

Lily nodded, determination on her face as she moved to have another go.

Then she jumped but rotated too early. She landed it, but barely, her hand pushing off the ice, so she didn't tumble.

Not that Lily cared. She spun toward Fanny and pumped her hands in the air. "I did it!"

"You did!" Fanny smiled, hugging her back when the girl threw her arms around Fan's waist. "Great job," she said.

"Someday I want to be able to do a triple."

"Someday," she said, tugging the end of her ponytail, "you'll be able to."

"You think so?"

"I believe in you."

Lily tossed a huge smile in her direction then went off to continue practicing.

Fanny started toward the exit for a second, only to be waylaid again. She saw some crossovers, a girl take her first strides without the aid of a bucket to hold her up, and then some snow angels. None of which she was getting paid to see. But that was okay. Because kids.

She really loved them.

Eventually, she managed to get off the ice and move toward the bench just inside the hall where her bag was stowed.

She had one skate off when she felt it.

The tendril of heat sliding down her nape.

Her eyes shot up, and there he was.

Striding up to her as though he hadn't made her come by dry-humping her in a public hallway, and then had left her, knees shaking, lips swollen, hair a fucking mess. She barely remembered stumbling into the stall and trying to put herself to rights, knowing that she looked like she'd been ravished. *Feeling* like she had been ravished . . . even while part of her wished that he'd torn her panties off, unzipped, and—

Fuck.

She'd eventually managed to peel herself out of the bathroom, looking somewhat put together, to find that Charlie had not only passed her dessert test, but fucking aced it. He'd ordered both chocolate cake *and* cheesecake, and not only that, while she'd been unleashing her dry-humping she-demon in the hall, he'd worried that she wasn't feeling well, so had asked the server to box them up.

Then had sent both home with her.

Then had followed her home, since they'd met at the brewery.

Then had walked her to the porch and kissed her on the cheek.

Then had fucking texted her to make sure she was feeling better the next morning.

The fuck?

Seriously. The man was wonderful.

And she was . . . orgasming courtesy of her ex, drooling over said ex, *dreaming* of him, and—

She was an asshole.

But she didn't have time to ponder the full extent of her assholeness before Brandon was crouching next to her and reaching for her skates.

"Don't," she hissed, jerking her feet away.

He lifted his hands, stayed crouched, but his face was gentle when he said, "Are you okay?"

Leveling a glare at him was her only answer before bending to unlace her skates and tug them off. She dried the blade, stashed them away, slipped her tired feet into her fuzzy boots, and stood before striding down the hall. Her car was parked out front and though this exit would put her farther from it, she was willing and able to take all escape routes.

"Fan," he said. "I should—"

She whipped toward him, narrowed her eyes. "If you're going to apologize, don't bother."

His brows lifted.

"I was just as much a part of that as you were."

He relaxed. She saw the tension bleed from his shoulders.

"But it was still wrong."

That tension snuck back in, tightening his jaw, flattening his lips. "It didn't feel wrong to me." He stepped closer, his lips finding her ear. "I came in my hand twice last night thinking about how fucking sexy you were wrapped around me."

Was there any oxygen left in the hallway?

Or had this man just stolen it all?

He'd never talked like that before, his husky voice, the sleek, muscled lines of his body so close to hers, bringing her right back to the previous night. She wanted him. She was two seconds away from jumping into his arms and wrapping her legs around him again, only this time with his cock *inside* her instead of against her. "Brandon," she breathed, shivering when he ran one rough fingertip down the side of her neck.

"What are you doing here?"

She jumped, probably looking guilty as hell.

Definitely *feeling* guilty as hell.

Her head jerked down the hall, seeing Kaydon walking toward her, though his eyes were on Brandon, and belatedly she remembered that it would be strange for Brandon to be here. Agents didn't just show up at practices, let alone show up twice in a week.

Brandon straightened slightly, and she watched him as he tucked the heat away, his expression going casual as he held up a folder she had completely missed.

Was he a fucking magician?

Where had he been keeping that?

"I had the signed contract from yesterday."

Kaydon studied Brandon for a long moment before he lifted a brow. "You couldn't email me?"

"I—"

Maybe it was cowardice. Maybe it was smart. Maybe . . . she just wanted to see what lengths Brandon would go to in order to follow her, to talk with her.

Would he chase her down? Catch her arm again?

So maybe it was another test, only instead of dessert, this time it was . . .

To see if he was interested? No. To see if he would forget her.

Or maybe it was all of that, twisted and tangled together along with the fear of letting him in again, but either way, when Kay asked Brandon to see the contract and then began asking questions, Fanny snagged her skate bag and hauled ass to the exit.

TWELVE

BRANDON

"I don't think she wants to talk to you," Kay said, closing the folder the moment Fanny was out of sight and fixing Brandon with an intense stare.

He turned to follow her.

Kaydon grabbed his arm, stalling him. "What are you doing, man?"

"Mind your own business." Brandon tried to shrug off his hand.

The fucker just held on. Damn hockey players and their giant hands. "Dude," Kay snapped, shaking him slightly. "What are you *doing?*"

"She's mine," Brandon hissed, finally managing to break Kaydon's grip. He started walking after her.

"Doesn't seem like she wants to be."

That had him stopping and turning around. "She's just scared because—"

Fuck. It was too complicated a conversation to have in this moment, especially when Kay didn't know any of their history.

"Scared why?" Kaydon's voice was deadly, his expression

doubly so, and Brandon had the notion that he was seeing what the other man's face might look like just before he mowed down an opponent on the ice. "What did you do?" His words grew even icier. "Did you hurt her?"

Brandon bit back a curse.

"Not like you're thinking," he said, and when Kaydon grabbed his shoulder, fingers digging in fiercely, Brandon knew that even though Kay was new to the Gold, Fanny had already earned his respect. Just as he knew Kaydon would throw down to protect her—and not just because she was a member of the Gold, but because Kay had seen the woman Fanny was, seen how much love and care she deserved.

Which was why he took thirty seconds to lay it out for him.

Kaydon already knew about the cancer. When Kay's mom had been diagnosed a couple of years ago, they'd talked it out, and Brandon had shared his own experience, but Kay didn't know about Fanny and everything that had gone down.

So, Brandon told him in those thirty seconds, understanding full well that the tale might end up on the Gold's gossip train, that the team might intervene, and the intervention might not be in his favor.

He wasn't a safe choice.

But given a chance, he would love Fanny with every fiber of his being. He would love her until he was in the ground, or until that love was forcibly taken away from him. Brandon couldn't make guarantees. Fuck knew, he'd lived enough life to understand that, but he also knew that he wouldn't let her go without a fight.

To do that, Kaydon needed to understand.

And maybe the rest of the team needed to understand that as well.

"Fuck," Kay breathed when Brandon finished his short, sharp explanation. "That's a fucking mess, man. You still love her?"

"I do," Brandon said, starting to move past Kaydon. He was probably already too late. Fan had probably already drifted off.

"And she still feels something for me. So, I'm not letting her go. I'm going to fight for her and—"

"And if she doesn't want that?"

Brandon stopped.

"Will you let her go?"

Brandon dropped his head, staring at his feet, knowing the answer and knowing it probably wasn't the one Kaydon wanted to hear. If Fanny wanted him to move on, to let go, he honestly wasn't sure he could respect that wish. He thought that he might fight for her until he didn't have breath in his lungs.

"Make damned sure that you understand what's in your heart before you make your way back into hers."

Brandon sighed. "Not going to warn me off?"

Kaydon's mouth turned up. "I think you already understand how well-liked Fanny is with the guys. You'll have enough people to warn you off when they realize who you're after." He clapped Brandon on the shoulder and pointed back toward the rink. "You might have a chance to catch her if you go out that way. She usually parks out front."

With a nod of thanks, Brandon left Kaydon in the hall, holding the contract he'd printed out and hand-delivered for no reason other than Kay had mentioned his session with Fanny at dinner last night.

Then he exited the rink, knowing that a battle was forthcoming.

And looking forward to every damned minute of it.

———

She was just getting into her car.

He sped up, saw the redhead who'd been talking to her slant a curious gaze in his direction, and then a smug smile, but he didn't stop to analyze either.

Instead, he snagged the car door before Fanny could close it.

"Hey," he said, casually, standing in the open frame.

Her hand was still on the door, her arm outstretched, her fingers wrapped around the smooth metal handle. His greeting had her sighing and then glancing up at him, her brow lifted. "Really?"

"Hi, baby," he murmured, crouching down and running his fingers lightly up her arm. "Is that better?"

She shivered, snatched her arm back. "No."

Amusement coiled through him, but he was starting to understand that her snapping at him was a good thing. It meant that she felt something, and even if that something at the moment was being annoyed with him, then he'd take it. Annoyance was better than distance. And it sure as shit was better than not feeling *anything* for him.

"You here to talk to me about your masturbation habits again?" she gritted out.

Shock had him freezing.

But then the moment of surprise rapidly transformed into pleasure. He grinned slowly. "You want me to tell you about them?" he murmured, leaning close, not missing how she inhaled sharply, how her hands clenched into fists, her knuckles standing out sharply against her skin. "I don't mind."

She exhaled, slow and steady, but her seemingly calm breathing was belied by the fact that her cheeks had gone rosy, her irises dilated. "Well, I do," she muttered.

"No"—a tug of her ponytail—"you don't." He smothered a grin. "Want me to tell you how I was so turned on that it barely took me three strokes to come?" he said, loving that her cheeks flushed further. "Or that it didn't even take the edge off, not when I could still taste you on my tongue, could imagine what your slick heat would feel like around me. So"—he leaned closer, not bothering to hide his smile when she shivered—"as soon as I came, I had to jerk off again."

"That's disgusting."

Her voice was so breathless that he knew she thought that was anything *but* disgusting.

"Liar," he murmured, so close now that his lips brushed her earlobe, that he couldn't resist nipping the delicate dangling bit of flesh.

She moaned.

"Did you make yourself come?"

"Wh-what?"

"After what I did to you in the restaurant, did you go home and make yourself come?"

"I—" She shook her head. He hadn't moved back, so her hair caught the stubble on his jaw, her scent filled his nose. "No, of course not."

"Liar," he murmured again and had the pleasure of seeing her cheeks go fire engine red.

"Brandon," she whispered.

"Yeah?"

Her eyes sparked as her hand found his chest, shoved him back so he landed on the warm pavement.

"You're an asshole."

She slammed the door, nearly clocking him in the head. The *click* of the lock engaging had him jumping to his feet.

"You can run," he said, knowing it probably wasn't loud enough for her to hear.

But she could read his lips, apparently.

Just like he could read hers.

Because he watched her mouth move, watched it form the words, "I'm not running."

So, for a third time, he said, "Liar."

Then she revved her engine and took off.

For some reason, he was grinning when she nearly mowed him over.

Maybe he loved to live dangerously.

Maybe he just loved her.

Thirteen

Fanny

Fury was her companion the whole way home.

Through the traffic.

Through the stop for gas.

Through pulling into her driveway and going inside, accompanying her as she ate dinner, as she finished off her bottle of wine.

How dare he?

Seriously, how fucking *dare* he?

She should have run his ass over in the parking lot. Things would have been so much simpler and—

Her phone rang.

Sighing, she moved to the counter and picked it up, and no—*fucking no!*—that wasn't disappointment sliding through her when the caller ID showed that it was Charlie calling her and not Brandon with more surprising sexy talk that he'd learned somewhere along the way.

Because he sure as shit hadn't had it when they'd been together.

Which meant that he'd learned it somewhere that wasn't with her. Which meant that he might have learned it from Angela.

That painful thought had her picking up the phone.

"Hey, beautiful," Charlie said, his warm voice making the fury that had gripped her for the last hour dissipate.

"Hey," she said, smiling as she leaned back against the counter.

"You feeling better?"

Ah. There was the pang of guilt.

She deserved it after her shenanigans in the hall. Or maybe, Brandon did. He was the instigator—and yes, she knew she'd been an active participant. Damn. She really *should* have run over the fucker.

"Fanny?" Charlie asked. "You there?"

"Yes." She straightened as though he could see her, as though she were on her best behavior and not thinking about Brandon and running him over . . . nor about how delicious his sexy talk had been. Shivering, she forced herself to focus. "I'm sorry. I'm here, and I'm feeling better. Thanks for asking."

"If this is a bad time, I can let you go."

More guilt.

Fuck.

"It's not."

"So, it's not a bad time, and you're feeling better." Charlie's words were light. "Then it must be that you're immune to my patented charm."

She laughed. "Yes, it's that exactly."

"Damn."

"Thanks for dinner last night," she told him. "I had a really nice time."

"I'm glad. I did, too. Now, stop with the niceties and give me all the gossip about my sister. What kind of trouble is Scar causing?"

"Your sister is an angel."

"And now I know what your voice sounds like when you're lying."

Her amusement boiled over, and she found herself giggling—actually *giggling*. Like a little girl. *Again*. Charlie was just so . . . Charlie. A bright ray of sunshine in her life. "You're just as bad as she is."

"Oh really?" he teased. "Tell me more."

"How dare you, good sir?" she countered. "I'd never betray my friends."

"Hmm. So, you're one of *those*."

She picked up her glass of wine. "Those?"

"One of those rule-followers."

"You got me," she said dryly.

"Don't worry, Scar and I will fix that for you." A beat. "Did Scarlett ever tell you about the time she tried to push me out a second-story window?"

Fanny found herself laughing again. "What? No."

"I was two. She was three, and she hated that all my cuteness usurped hers. So, she . . ."

And then he spun a wild tale about a three-year-old Scar somehow plotting murder because he'd gotten more hugs from their grandmother than she had that day. She called him on his bullshit, and he readily admitted that it was just that—*bullshit*—before telling her that it was a bizarre and terrible accident, but that luckily he hadn't been seriously hurt.

As she listened to him, she had the notion that this is what it could be like with Charlie. He would make her laugh, and their conversations wouldn't be filled with tension and the painful past, with guilt and wishing things would have turned out differently.

They would just be light and fresh and . . . easy.

They talked for a long time, and all the while it was tempting, *so* tempting to continue to lean into the feeling he created within her, to pretend that Brandon didn't exist, and that she could be this woman, be the person she was with Charlie—whole, light, carefree—all the time.

But she couldn't ignore Brandon, couldn't pretend he didn't exist.

And she knew that she wouldn't ever be able to be fully present with Charlie, not in the way he deserved.

Which was why when he asked her out to dinner the following night, her answer was, "I can't."

Silence.

It wasn't fair to him, for her to be hung up on another man. He deserved more, so much more than she could give him.

"Ah," he said quietly, sober for the first time since they'd first begun talking. "Is it because of Scarlett? I promise I would never get in between your friendship."

"It's—" She broke off before she blabbed her entire sob story. "It's not about Scar," she said.

"I see."

"It's not you, it's . . . damn"—she sighed and shook her head —"I don't mean it like that. I'm just not in the right mental head-space for a relationship. There's someone from my past, and it's complicated, and I can't be with anyone while it's still so unsettled."

"I understand," he said gently. "No hard feelings."

"Would you—" Cutting herself off before she could ask. It wasn't fair.

"Would I what?"

Another shake of her head, even though he couldn't see her.

"Fanny," he ordered. "Just ask."

She winced then blurted, "Would you want to be friends?" God, that sounded stupid and juvenile, and she wanted to grab the words out of the air and shove them back into her mouth.

Silence for a heartbeat too long, then, "Of course, I would."

"You don't have to—"

"You're a cool chick, Fanny. Gorgeous, funny, and talented," he said, and she felt her cheeks heat. "So, even if you're not inter-ested in me, I'd love to be friends." A chuckle. "Plus, if I can keep you nearby, I might get a second crack at dating you."

Laughter had her shaking her head. "You're—"

"Unbelievable in the best way possible?"

"That wasn't exactly what I was thinking."

Unfazed, he said, "Let's go to dinner. As friends," he added when she began to protest.

"As friends," she agreed.

"Perfect. That means I still have a shot to squeeze out more dirt from you about Scarlett."

———

By the time she got off the phone with Charlie, she was pleasantly buzzed.

They'd chatted and joked, and he'd given her several good blackmail stories about Scarlett that had Fan nearly in tears and looking forward to her newfound friendship.

Charlie was good people.

Eventually, though, she'd yawned, and Charlie had told her he'd see her in a few days at the charity raffle then had ordered her to get to sleep.

She was tired but not sleepy, so she went to the kitchen for more wine, topping off her glass and parking her ass on the couch. There was a new horror show she wanted to jump into, and tonight seemed as good a time as any to start.

The knock came when she was fully immersed in the show and at a particularly tense moment.

She jumped, nearly upending her wine, her heart pounding like a motherfucker.

"Shit," she gasped, clamping her free hand over her chest then glaring toward the front door.

The knock came again.

Probably, someone trying to sell her something.

Well, good for that person. She wasn't getting her ass off the couch. Lifting the remote, she turned up the volume and kept watching.

Whoever was on the other side of the door didn't get the hint. They knocked again. Louder and longer. She sighed, glanced at the clock, and realized it was late. *Really* late. Of course, it wouldn't be someone selling something. This was a different kind of visit.

And considering the persistence, as the knocking continued, she had a suspicion who it was.

"Fuck," she muttered. So much for not getting off her couch. Sighing, she hit the button to pause her show and stood up, making it to the front door just as there was yet another knock, this one near-pounding, instead of the medium-level tapping from before.

She whipped open the door.

And sighed.

In annoyance, not in pleasure. Not because the man looked fucking delicious standing on her porch in a pair of low-slung jeans that looked as soft as butter along with a tight blue sweater. He was holding a large basket, and she could see an inch of taut, golden skin exposed by his sweater having risen up.

"Hi, beautiful," he murmured, and she snapped her eyes up to his. Away from the temptation of the shadows of squares she could just barely make out, away from that peekaboo of his flat abdomen.

"What are you doing here?"

"I have something for you."

She frowned, wondered exactly why the hell he'd show up on her porch bearing gifts after . . . "I nearly ran you over with my car," she blurted.

He grinned, the fool. "Maybe I like that."

"You've lost it," she muttered, backing up, intending to slam the door closed.

But the fucker stepped forward instead, striding over the threshold and into her house, saying, "Thanks, I *will* come in."

And for all that she talked and instructed for a living,

Brandon barreling his way into her entryway had her sputtering. "I—I—"

He walked right by her, disappearing into the kitchen.

"I—"

A car drove by, the headlights flashing past her front yard, and Fanny realized that she was just standing there, staring at the empty hall, the open door. Blinking, she closed and locked the door then turned and followed Brandon.

He was unpacking the basket on her kitchen counter.

"What the hell are you doing?"

"Here," he said, thrusting the basket at her.

She scrambled to take it, the contents within rattling, and she glanced down to see they were all wrapped. Then repeated her question. "Seriously, what the hell are you doing?"

A smile, before he spun away and began searching through her cabinets until he located a vase, plunking a large arrangement of sunflowers into it after he'd filled it with water.

"Cooking you dinner."

"It's after nine."

He lifted a brow. "Have you eaten?"

No, she hadn't. She'd been on the phone through dinner with Charlie, and truthfully, she was never great at eating dinner. She never had been. Oftentimes, she got lost in some task or show, and then she forgot to eat.

Plus, it was nearly bedtime. It was never good to eat at bedtime.

She was more of a breakfast person, mostly because she sometimes got so busy on the ice that she forgot to eat lunch, too. But anyway, that was beside the point. Breakfast was the shit. Give her a donut or a muffin or a croissant, and she was a happy girl.

"Right," Brandon said, turning back to the bag and continuing to unload what looked to be way too much food for two people.

"Do you think I have a hollow leg?" she muttered.

"I'm hungry. You've always been the type of girl to eat," he said, pulling out a package of chicken breasts. "I'm guessing that hasn't changed. Plus, you're too thin."

Her mouth dropped open, her gaze sliding down her body and making her realize that she was still holding the basket. "I am *not!*" she snapped, tossing the basket on the island.

"You're thinner than when you were skating."

Jaw clenching, she said, "I don't have that extra muscle."

"Bullshit," he told her. "You're plenty strong. You just don't remember to eat, and you don't have someone to take care of you."

"I—"

He set down a head of lettuce and crossed to her. "This is me telling you I'm going to take care of you."

She inhaled. Sharply.

He was close. Really close.

Which meant her inhale had the disastrous effect of bringing her breasts flush against his chest. Worse. Her inhale had her nipples brushing against his chest, heat scorching down her spine, moisture flooding her pussy, and making her suck in another breath.

Which just made the cycle worse.

Breathe. Brush. Pleasure.

And not once did Brandon back off.

His hand came to her cheek, cupped it gently, lightly running his thumb over her lips. "You've spent too many years without someone to take care of you. I'm not letting any more time pass without doing that."

Her lips parted.

A breath shuddered out.

Brandon's eyes went hot, his thumb pressed slightly more firmly against her bottom lip. His head came down . . .

He straightened, nudged her back, and returned to making himself at home in her kitchen. "Open your presents," he said as he bent and pulled out a pan.

Fanny blinked.

A long, slow blink.

She turned back to the basket, which was indeed filled with presents.

Another blink, her gaze rotating to Brandon again.

Who was still there, now pulling a cutting board out and getting busy with the lettuce.

"Fan?"

He'd moved on to the chicken, using a different cutting board as he coated them in some seasoning he must have brought because she didn't have anything in her house aside from olive oil, salt, and pepper.

"Yeah?" she asked, watching him put some oil in the pan.

"Open the presents."

She nibbled at the corner of her mouth, hesitating, but then, ultimately, she reached into the basket and picked up the first wrapped package. For one, she loved presents. For another . . . she loved presents. Smiling, she carefully began peeling back the tape, slowly removing it so that she could savor the experience. She didn't receive presents. She hadn't shared her birthday with her friends, and her parents . . . well, celebrating that day wasn't on their agenda.

The Gold went all out on Christmas, but she always timed her vacation for then, making sure to be out of sight and mind for the celebrations.

Actually thinking about it now, the last time she'd received a present from anyone was when Grace had sent her a pair of cozy pajamas for Christmas before she'd passed away. The memory had her fingers faltering, the present resting on the counter as she blinked rapidly.

Fingers on her chin. "What is it?" Brandon asked gently.

She should have lied, pretended she was fine. But, for some reason, the words came anyway. "I miss your mom," she whispered.

He went quiet and still.

And then his arms slipped around her, tugged her close. "I know," he murmured. "I do, too."

He held her for a few moments and then stepped away, returning to the pan, putting in the chicken. As it sizzled, he went to the sink and washed up. She focused on the present as he turned to continue with whatever else he was making, and she finally made some progress on the paper, getting all the tape off and then slowly peeling it open.

"Oh," she breathed, touching the soft blue ombre scarf that reminded her of the bright cerulean, cloudless sky meeting the turquoise waves of the ocean.

"Do you like it?"

"It's beautiful," she said truthfully, running her finger over the delicate material. "I—" She broke off, unsure what she wanted to ask.

Okay, that was a lie.

She knew what she wanted to ask.

She was just too much of a coward to say it out loud.

Brandon wiped his hands on a towel, came over, and plucked another present from the basket. "Open this one next."

She didn't hesitate this time, just carefully pulled open the paper, revealing an expensive box of sea salt caramels. "How—"

He was there again, reaching into the basket, handing her an envelope.

Fanny didn't have the same compunction to save envelopes that she had to save pretty wrapping paper, so she tore into it and tugged out the card.

I have ten years to make up for. This is just a start.

"I'd planned on making sure you didn't open that before I left," he murmured, tugging out the paper that she hadn't realized was taped inside the card and handing it to her. "But I decided I wanted to see your face when you do."

Frowning, she unfolded the printout and felt her mouth drop open.

It was a reservation to a winery north of them. The same winery they'd planned on getting married at.

She didn't know how she felt about that.

"It's for two," he said, moving to the pan and flipping the chicken. "But only if you want it to be. It can just as easily be for one." He glanced up, but she couldn't decipher his expression, not when she was so surprised, not when her mind was swirling. "I just thought that you might want to wipe the slate clean and start over. A fresh start. Something we can experience together and—"

She put her hand up.

He stopped talking.

Her mind continued spinning.

"Why?" she asked.

"Because I love you."

If she'd thought her mind was swirling before, then she had no notion of the idea. Because *now* her mind was swirling, spinning faster and faster until her head felt like it was going to ratchet right off her neck. Her emotions were all over the place—joy and fear, hope and terror, desire and longing. They were all twisted up, and yet, the one thing she couldn't stop from coming to the forefront of her mind, the *one* emotion that overshadowed all the others, was love.

She had never stopped loving this man.

But she couldn't say *that*. Just the thought of being that vulnerable to him had her throat constricting, her pulse pounding in her veins, sweat breaking out on her upper lips. Her fingers clenched on the paper, her gaze unseeing as she tried not to hyperventilate.

She didn't know how long she stood there, shock and panic roiling just beneath her skin, but the next thing she was aware of was warm fingers stroking down her arm, tugging the paper from her fingers, a gentle hand nudging her toward the counter where a plate of food now sat.

"Eat, honey," he said. "I'm sorry about the trip. That was too soon."

The vise on her lungs eased slightly. "Brandon," she said. "I don't think we can start over. I'm not sure a clean slate will ever be possible. There's just too much between us."

"Then we don't start over, we move forward."

She scoffed. "It's not that easy. I—" She faltered, not knowing what she wanted, whether she wanted to keep moving forward with Brandon, or to cut things off once and for all. To give in to the longing, or to shore up the walls around her and stay safe.

He cupped the side of her neck. "We don't have to do this tonight."

"But—"

"All of this will hold."

Her eyes flew to his. "I—" She shook her head, knew that she wouldn't come to any conclusions tonight. The answers weren't simple. They never would be, and . . . she sighed because he was right. All of this would hold. She could take some time to think, to sort out what she wanted to do, or time to admit to herself . . .

Not. Tonight.

"Right," she murmured.

He smiled, and it filled her stomach with butterflies. Then he lightly pressed on her shoulder, coaxing her onto the stool. "Food."

She sat.

He passed her a fork. She scooped up a bite.

"That's my girl," he murmured, kissing her temple and sitting down next to her. On her left side, because he was a leftie, and sitting there meant that he could lace their hands together and they could both still eat.

Fanny held her breath, wondering if he remembered.

But a heartbeat later, she wondered why part of her thought he hadn't.

Because his warm, rough fingers intertwined with hers . . . and then he asked her about the show that was paused on her TV.

They ate and held hands and talked about the show then talked about everything and nothing.

There wasn't any angst or stress or painful memories.

It was just the two of them.

And for the hour he stayed before kissing her on the forehead, before he wished her a soft, "Good night," and headed out the front door, Fan felt like she was fourteen again.

Fourteen and in love with Brandon Cunningham.

———

The first game of the season was in less than a week, and the hockey boys sure cleaned up nice.

She didn't often get to see them in their big kid clothes.

And it was a damned good view.

"You look nice."

Fanny jumped as Charlie came up next to her. The man had serious ninja skills, but that wasn't what had kept Fanny running around the entire afternoon, setting up tall tables for people to gather, talk, and eat (and drink because the more they drank, the more they would spend), hanging decorations, checking in with the caterers and the bartenders, fixing a strand of twinkly lights when they'd gone out. No, that was all Scar and her clipboard filled with never-ending tasks.

Fan had hauled planters of live plants from the truck outside into the large auditorium, had positioned and re-positioned them until Scar had been satisfied there were enough intimate corners to encourage conversation but not enough to be a hookup zone.

Hookups did not bring money to the charity.

There was a long list of things that didn't bring money to the charity, and Scar had told Fanny all of them.

When Scar had finally released her from setup duty, Fan all

but ran into the bathroom to wash her sweaty face, slap on some deodorant and makeup, pull on her dress, slip into heels.

Now, with barely ten minutes before guests were supposed to show up, she'd tossed Scar a hundred dollars for her donation and finally felt like she had a moment to breathe and admire the space she'd had a hand in setting up before she had to man her station and serve up drinks.

All she could say was that Scarlett was a genius.

Charlie had been commandeered to hang sheer swathes of fabric along the walls—Fan had hung the twinkly lights behind, fussing with them until Scar had been happy. Combined with the tables and flowers and plants, not to mention, even *more* strands of lights, the entire space seemed otherworldly.

A fairy garden brought to life.

And if Scar had her way, there would be plenty of revelry, enough anyway to open those pocketbooks.

"You look nice yourself," she told Charlie, tearing her gaze away from the decor, from where the guys were strolling through the door and positioning themselves at the various tables, readying to schmooze and get that money.

It was true—the whole looking nice thing.

Charlie had done some changing of his own, swapping the jeans and tee for a sleek black suit, his crisp white shirt making his skin look tan and strokable. The fit was tight, showing off the lean strength of his shoulders and thighs.

He smiled at her perusal.

And she narrowed her eyes in return. He knew just how attractive he was.

Too bad she couldn't appreciate it fully. He was like a lovely piece of artwork, but he didn't set her blood on fire.

"What job does Scar have you doing?" she asked.

"Manning the silent auction," he said. "You?"

"Bartend—" Fan started to answer him, but then her skin began prickling, her gaze drawn back to the door.

To the *man* walking through the door.

Sweet baby Jesus, now *that* was a suit.

If she'd thought that Charlie's fit him like a glove then Brandon's . . . hell, he might as well be naked for how well it was tailored. She could see the outline of his thighs, his torso, his arms, his abs—

He turned to say something to Kaydon, and she nearly groaned at the way the material hugged his ass.

She loved his ass.

She had loved it when they were together, loved looking at it, or even grinning as she gave it a slight smack when he went by. Because he was hers and she could touch him whenever she wanted, but she had especially loved holding on to it when he plunged deep inside her, gripping him tight so he could grind against her clit and—

Fan blinked, forced her gaze away, definitely not feeling fourteen any longer.

No, she was feeling like a woman—*all* woman—and that woman wanted the man who'd bought her favorite treat—the sea salt caramels—her favorite flowers—the sunflowers. The man who gifted the beautiful scarf to remind her of the ocean and the peace she felt there. The man who'd cooked for her and whose body she could taste every inch of while stripping that sexy as hell suit off—

Charlie shifted next to her, breaking her sexual haze. "Ah."

"What?"

His gaze flickered from her face and deliberately slid to where Brandon had spotted them and was approaching, his expression falling decidedly on the side of displeased. A coil of heat slid through her as she remembered the hall, him telling her to get rid of Charlie. She wouldn't, of course. She liked Charlie and had spent enough time living her own life to ignore orders from a *man,* even if that man was Brandon. "*That's* the complicated ex."

Mouth dropping open, she tore her gaze from Brandon and turned to Charlie. "That's not—"

Charlie leveled a glance at her. "I thought we were friends now."

"We are."

"Then save that bullshit for someone else."

Her lips pressed flat, shoulders falling slightly, and she sighed, admitted. "Fine. He's the complication."

Before Brandon reached them, Scarlett came up, snagging his arm and dragging him to a halt as she jabbered his ear off. Brandon nodded, apparently listening. But his eyes were on Fanny . . . and Charlie, fury flaring across his face as he looked at the two of them standing close together.

"Damn, he's scary," Charlie muttered, grinning at her. "So, why is he complicated?"

Another sigh. "It's too *complicated* to get into."

"Promise to tell me over tequila shots and nachos?" he asked.

Shuddering, she said, "No tequila. Not ever."

"Rum?"

"With nachos?"

His smile didn't fade. "Obviously."

"Well, then," she said. "That I can do."

"Good." He tugged a lock of her hair. "I'll hold you to that." He started to step back then glanced over his shoulder, moved close, and bent so that his next words puffed against the shell of her ear. "For the record, given the way he looks at you and his obvious wish to murder me for being this close to you, I say get over *complicated* and throw the man a bone."

"I—"

"Because I think a man like that could give you a good one."

Her mouth fell open again, and hell, that was becoming a habit.

One that continued when he straightened, winked, said, "I'm bi, but even if I wasn't, I could appreciate the scenery." He kissed her cheek, her damn jaw having dropped open again, and disappeared.

It only took her a moment to realize why.

Brandon.

As in, Brandon was *there*, in front of her, his fury radiating off him, forcing the space to go taut, her skin to prickle, her pussy . . . to get wet.

Maybe it was wrong, but she really, *really* liked it when Brandon got all possessive.

It was a new side of him, and that newness had her thinking that a future might be possible, that they might be able to discover new things about each other, build something fresh and unmarred and . . . *them*.

He crossed his arms.

She found herself leaning close, not missing when his eyes dipped, dropping to the deep V of her dress, to the cleavage that was on full display—part because Scar had said it would help her with the whole selling booze and thus people getting drunker and spending more money thing, but also because Fanny liked herself, liked her body, and she didn't mind showing off the curves she had.

Even if Brandon thought she was too thin.

Her breasts brushed against his chest as she rose on tiptoe, her mouth coming very close to his, bypassing it at the last moment before she stretched farther and whispered in his ear, "You still think I'm too skinny?"

His breath shot out of him in a whoosh, his fingers came to her hips, but before he could get a good grip, she spun away and walked to her station, saying over her shoulder, "Oh, by the way, you look damned good in that suit."

And if there was a bit of sway in her hips as she did so, then . . . there was a bit of sway in her hips.

The man had opened the door.

He'd shown her the possibilities.

He'd made her wonder and hope that he'd be there to catch her if she fell.

Well, he'd better have his glove ready because she was thinking she might finally be ready to leap.

FOURTEEN

BRANDON

Holy hell, what had he unleashed?

It took every bit of self-control he possessed to not follow after her, to not chase her down, toss her over his shoulder, and find out if that little display of flirting meant what he hoped to fuck it did.

Was she going to give him a chance to win her back?

She slipped behind a bartending station, and he moved to it, not caring that Scarlett had ordered him to make the rounds.

He didn't give a fuck about the charity, not when Fanny was there. His gaze dipped when she bent to scoop up some ice, giving him a full view down her dress, one he enjoyed, but one that also made him want to tear off his jacket and wrap it around her so no one else could see her breasts encased in black silk.

Then she straightened and plunked a glass in front of him.

Brandon blinked. "A Manhattan?" he asked after lifting the drink to his lips and taking a sip.

"Is it still your favorite?"

His mouth curved. "Yeah, baby, it is." He reached over the bar top and snagged her hand. "Does you talking to me mean that . . ."

"That I'm going to give us another chance?" she asked.

He nodded.

"No."

His heart sank.

"But it means I'm considering it." She slipped her hand away, turned to smile at a woman who came up for a drink. "Especially, if you keep dressing like that."

Hope bloomed in his chest.

She turned and helped the woman, whipping up drinks like she belonged behind the bar.

"How'd you get so good at slinging drinks?" he asked.

Fan measured off a shot of vodka and began mixing it with cranberry juice, pouring both into a martini glass and accepting the cash from the woman. She stuffed it into a jar and then turned back to him. "When the tour ended, I bartended before my skating business took off." A shrug. "It was fun, and I like talking to people. Plus, I learned how to mix a lot of drinks." She winked. "I'm really fun at parties."

"I know you are."

Just as he knew that *this* was the Fanny he remembered. Beautiful and bright and happy. But more settled, comfortable in her own skin, and able to strike a mean conversation.

All that press, and he supposed, also the bartending made it so she didn't skip a beat as more people made their way to the bar, and she started pulling glasses and pouring liquor nearly as fast and furious as her words came. She charmed and chatted and pretty soon, there was a line of customers at her station.

She glanced at him—a sly look out of the corner of her eye—and said, "You going to stand there staring all night? Or you going to get back here and help?"

More hope.

He drained his glass, slipped behind the bar, and pressed a kiss to the side of her neck, loving that she didn't push him away, loving the scent of her, loving . . . *her.*

"Tell me what to do."

"You take care of wine and beer," she said, nodding at the bottles behind them. "I'll do the rest."

He nodded. "I can do that."

She smirked. "We'll see."

And then things really got going. Fan glanced up at the man in front of them and took his order—two red wines, one beer—and then the woman behind him—two cosmos, one beer, one white wine—and Brandon promptly felt himself begin to scramble.

That scrambling didn't stop.

The next hour was more of the same. He was sweating, his arms exhausted, his brain fried from having to take money and make change by the time the line tapered off and people had gone from their first to second to third round of drinks. There was still a trickle of attendees coming up to the bar, but they had thinned out, giving him a moment to breathe and also to go back to staring.

She was gorgeous.

And funny and smart and really fucking good at mixing drinks.

"Is there anything you can't do?"

She lifted a rack of glasses—one he took from her and set on the table behind them. "Thanks," she murmured. "And yes, there are loads of things I can't do, things I suck at."

He slipped his arm around her waist. "Lies."

For a moment, she leaned back against him. "Okay, you're right. I'm brilliant at everything I take up, and I definitely, *definitely* don't have a closet that's overloaded with old clothes and needs to be organized, or always forget to take my car in for an oil change, or really, really suck at cross-stitch."

Brandon ran his fingers through the soft waves tumbling down her shoulder. "Cross-stitch?"

"I wanted a hobby." A shrug. "Turns out, I'm only good at making knots."

He bent, kissed her cheek. "Want me to make *you* a drink?"

A wide smile, warm eyes on him, her body melting back against his. She smelled like roses and vanilla. She smelled like *home*. She *felt* like home, there in his arms. "Okay," she said, and he realized his mistake because his offer had her slipping out of his hold. But then she was looking at him expectantly and with challenge in her eyes.

"Well," he murmured, "I know you like wine."

"Pft. Going the easy way out?" she teased.

"But," he said, talking over her. "I have a feeling that you're a straightforward drink kind of girl." He glanced at her, but her face was unreadable. "Not tequila," he murmured, remembering the hangovers they'd both gotten the first time they'd experimented with alcohol. Her expression didn't change, but her eyes warmed. He picked up a bottle of rum, used the shot glass measuring thingy to pour her a drink. One part of rum, and the rest of the glass with Coke and ice.

He handed it to her, watched as she sipped.

"Well?" he asked when she set it down.

Her lips curved. "It's a decent rum and Coke."

"Decent?" He wrapped his arms around her. "Just *decent?*"

A shrug that brought her breasts against him. A shrug that someone might interpret as casual, except for the hard nipples against his chest, the heat in her eyes. "Just decent," she repeated, her lips curving up, and it wasn't the time or place for it, but her mouth was tipped up, and her smile was sexy and—

He had to kiss her.

So, he did.

And then felt that hope inside him cover him from head to toe when she didn't hesitate to kiss him back.

———

Scar had interrupted the kiss, pulling Brandon away so he couldn't distract her best bartender.

"And the raffle is getting ready to start," she said. "You'll need to pull your ticket so I can make the announcement."

He nodded, started toward the table holding the huge glass bowls, most of which were now overflowing with raffle tickets.

Scarlett caught his arm.

"Also, if you hurt my friend again, I will chop off your balls, freeze them in those giant ice cube holders, and then shatter them with a hammer."

Brandon's brows lifted. "You're violent."

"I know it's not your fault. But"—she patted his cheek—"balls, hammer, shattered into pieces." A smile. "Don't forget it."

He shuddered. "Don't worry, I won't."

She led him to the tables, pointed out his bowl, and then had him reach in and pull out a ticket without looking at it.

"Thank you," she sing-songed, snagging it from his fingers, before flitting off to the microphone and quieting the crowd as he made his way back toward Fanny. Scar hadn't threatened his balls if he distracted Fanny, so he was going to make the most of their evening.

He slid behind the bar, wrapped an arm around her waist, and started to bend over to resume their kiss when he heard his name over the speakers.

". . . For dinner with a successful sports agent, Brandon Cunningham, VP at Prestige Media Group—"

Fan swatted him. "You're a raffle prize?" she asked.

"It's a long story. I'm helping out a friend."

". . . Insights from one of the best in the business, and he'll even pay the tab." The crowd laughed. "Our first prize winner of the evening is . . . Stephanie Douglas!"

The crowd applauded.

Brandon went stiff, though not as stiff as Fan. He glanced down at her, took in the shock on her face, the clenched jaw, he said, "I'm guessing you didn't enter for my raffle prize."

Her eyes narrowed. "No."

"Who—"

He didn't have to finish the question. "Ah. Scarlett at work."

Fanny nodded brusquely.

His lips tipped up. "Good thing I'd already planned to take you to dinner. Two birds, one stone."

Her eyes flashed. "We're not going on a date."

His brows lifted. "We're not?"

She pushed out of his hold. "No, we're not. I can't. We can't—"

"We are *so* going on a date," he said, snagging her again. "Whether it's from Scarlett's intervention or of our own volition."

A huff. "I'm going to—"

"Kiss me. And then go on a date with me."

"That's not happening," she growled, swatting at his chest. "I can't believe Scar did that. She needs to pick another ticket. It's not fair. I didn't enter for the prize, and someone else is going to miss out, and—"

He slanted his lips over hers, kissed her until they were both breathless.

"Go on a date with me," he said. Or maybe begged.

Either way, it seemed to do the trick.

She softened. "Okay to the date, but no to the stealing a prize from someone who paid good money to be here and—"

"You're accepting it."

Brandon managed to tear his gaze from Fanny and glanced over at Scarlett.

"That's not fair—"

Scar reached out and snagged Fanny from Brandon's arms. She dropped her hands onto Fanny's shoulders and shook her lightly. "Life has dealt you more than your fair share of unfair. You're accepting this. You're going on a date with Brandon, and you're going to have a good time."

"But someone else might want—"

Scarlett just crossed her arms and waited.

Fanny sighed. "You're not going to change your mind, are you?"

"No." Scar glared. "I don't care if you throw a fit. You're still going to do this. Not for me, for yourself. No more waffling and worrying, just *go* for it. Go for what you want."

"You're a terrible friend," Fan muttered.

"I love you, too," Scarlett said, completely undeterred by the muttering, "but you're *still* doing this."

Fanny's eyes drifted up to his, as though expecting to find an answer in them, but Brandon wasn't going to touch that with a ten-foot pole. This was between her and her friend. He'd already gotten his date. He couldn't give a shit about it being the raffle prize, or having to have another dinner with another prizewinner.

Sighing, reading his reluctance to dive in, she turned back to Scar. "What are you doing?"

Scarlett leaned in and spoke in her ear, saying something that Brandon couldn't hear. Whatever it was, it seemed to have the desired effect because Fanny's expression settled and softened. She pulled back, nodded, and then hugged Scar.

A moment later, Scarlett had drifted away, probably to cause more chaos somewhere else. Or well, not chaos, but to do whatever it took to get that money.

He sidled up to Fanny, slid an arm around her waist.

She didn't pull away and that, more than anything else, was the biggest victory of the night. There was a chance at a future with her.

"So," he murmured, running his fingers down her throat, "where should we go for our date tomorrow?"

"To—tomorrow?"

"Tomorrow," he repeated, nuzzling her throat.

He had this in, the door was nudged a little wider, and he wasn't going to give her the chance to slam it closed.

Fifteen

Fanny

She was exhausted.

It was the evening after the raffle, she'd hardly slept the night before, and only part of that was because of Scar's shenanigans the previous evening.

The rest was nerves.

She'd driven home and laid in bed and hadn't been able to sleep for hours.

It was so easy to be confident when all the yumminess of Brandon was in her vicinity, to lean into him when he slid an arm around her waist, to kiss him back when his lips found hers, but when he wasn't there and she was in her bed alone, under the covers, and all was quiet, the old doubts had decided to creep in.

What if he got sick again?

What if he *forgot* again?

What if she got her heart broken again?

What if—

The scenarios were endless . . . and terrifying.

She'd been up until the sun had begun to rise, unable to sleep until she'd finally given in and walked to the kitchen, grabbing the scarf Brandon had given her, wrapping the only piece of him she had in her possession around her, and that was what it had taken for her finally fall asleep.

Obviously, she'd slept the day away, thanking God it was Saturday and she had no clinics to teach and could laze in bed.

Now, she was still in her bedroom, having gorged herself on caramels while she was getting ready for her date. Probably, she should deliberately dress all frumpy, just because he'd been so presumptuous with the whole date-asking, taking advantage of her being so discombobulated to get her to agree, but she couldn't bring herself to do it. She wanted to bring her A-game.

She wanted his eyes to pop out of his head.

She wanted him to look at her with the tangle of heat and need that had danced across his dark brown eyes the night before.

So . . . she'd brought her A-game.

Sleek black stockings that stopped at mid-thigh. A lavender garter belt that she'd bought on a whim and never worn, the thin elastic bands making her shiver where they pressed into the skin on the front and back of her legs. Her bra was hardly more than a scrap of lace with absolutely no support. It looked pretty and the material brushed over her already sensitive nipples, causing desire to pool in her abdomen, moisture to flood her pussy.

The man wasn't even here yet, and she wanted him.

Desperately.

Her hands shook as she stepped into her dress and tugged up the zipper, thankful that it was under her arm, and she wasn't forced to contort herself to get it pulled up.

Then she was stepping into her stilettos, knowing her feet would be killing her in no time at all.

Worth it.

They made her legs look long and lean, and paired with her gorgeous black dress with its plunging neckline, short hem, and barely-there back, she knew she looked good. Combined with the full face of makeup, fake lashes, and long, loose curls down her back, she felt ready to take on the world when the doorbell rang.

She hustled to her bedroom and brushed her teeth in record time, thankful that her lipstick was the smudge-free variety, then moved downstairs and to the door . . . just as the bell rang again.

"Impatient," she muttered, reaching to open it.

"Sorry," Brandon said the moment it swung wide. "I wasn't sure you'd heard the—holy fucking shit." His jaw dropped open —literally open—and damn, that felt great for a number of reasons. First, she wasn't the one with her mouth gaping open, ready to catch flies. For another, she got that tangle of heat and need. And lastly, his throat worked for a long moment before he spoke again, his voice all sexy rasp that slid over her exposed skin. "You are so fucking beautiful."

"Yeah?" she whispered.

"Yeah." He reached for her then stopped, as though he didn't know where he could touch her.

If he could touch her.

She helped him cross that hurdle by stepping forward, not stopping until her body was flush with his. He looked good, too. Great, actually. He was wearing another one of those suits, and it showcased his long, lean lines. Mouthwateringly so.

But then she was against him and could see nothing but the strong delineation of his jaw, the soft cushions of his lips, the deep brown of his eyes.

He had a scar to the right of his eyebrow, one she hadn't seen before, and she found herself reaching up and brushing her thumb over it. "What happened?" she whispered. He hadn't had it when they'd been together.

His hand came up and covered hers, the roughness of his fingertips making her lean more heavily against him.

"I *should* tell you I got into a bar fight," he murmured, his words ruffling her hair.

"Or stopped a little old lady from getting mugged?" She played along.

"Then saved a stray kitten from a tree?"

She nodded, shifting back enough to see his eyes, her lips

curving upward when she saw the amusement dancing through those chocolate depths. "Exactly," she said, slowly sliding her fingers down his temple, his cheek, his jaw, his throat until her palm rested on his shoulder. "So, you clearly won the fight, saved the old lady, and rescued the kitten, and . . . ?"

"Ran into a cabinet I didn't close?" he chimed in.

Fanny froze. Then busted out laughing. "Seriously?" she asked through her guffaws.

"Unfortunately, yes." He pushed back a lock of hair that had fallen into her face. "But I got six stitches *and* a lesson in why I should close them."

"But the question is *do* you close them?"

A grin. "Yes, I learned that lesson, I promise."

"Glad to hear my head is safe."

He smiled down at her. "Should we go to dinner?"

Fan nodded, started to step out of his arms, then realized how much she hated the idea of not being held by him, even for just a couple of hours while they drove to the restaurant and ate. "Brandon?" she asked softly.

"Yeah, baby?" he asked, smoothing his hand over her hair.

"Do you want to go to dinner?"

His hand stopped, just for a moment, before weaving into her hair and gently tilting her head back. "Do *you* want to go to dinner?"

She shook her head.

"Thank fuck," he muttered.

Shock had her blinking at him as he backed her into the house and shut the door behind him. *Click* went the lock. Then his mouth was on hers. She gasped, and he took advantage, slipping his tongue inside and kissing her until she forgot about the fact that her feet were already pinching in her heels, that her lungs needed air, that her heart threatened to pound out of her chest.

When he broke away, her pulse was thundering in her veins, her breathing in rapid gusts.

"Why . . . thank . . . fuck?" she gasped.

He grinned, not even out of breath when she was feeling like she'd run a goddamn marathon. "Because I don't have to fight off all the other fuckers who would be looking at you tonight."

That had her straightening, her brows dragging together. "I hope you're not being serious."

He just kissed her again until her lungs threatened to burst, until she forgot what she'd been saying, until her outrage—and okay, a little bit of pleasure—at his possessiveness was a long lost thought.

"Do you want me to cook you dinner?" he asked when he'd released her lips.

It was so silken, so quiet that it took her a moment to process. "Um, what?"

"Are you hungry?"

She was hungry for sure. But dinner was the last thing on her mind. But wait, she needed to remember what had sparked her annoyance a moment before. What was it? Oh—

"You're not going to tell me how to dress," she said, jabbing a finger into his chest. He'd hadn't tried to before, but this was a different Brandon in a lot of ways—older, stronger, more intense —and she needed to set him straight right off the bat. If she wanted to run around San Francisco naked during Bay to Break-ers, she damn well could. If she wanted to wear her sexy dress and not care who looked, then she damned well would.

"Of course not."

The matter-of-fact way he said it took the wind out of her sails. She'd just been getting her mad on, and he responded with the correct answer.

"Oh," she said.

"But I'm not going to pretend that I don't have a claim."

That made her brows lift.

"Is that going to be a problem?" he asked.

Fanny should say it was going to be, just out of principal. She was a strong, independent woman. The only one with a claim over her was *her*. But . . . she couldn't lie and say a tiny part of her wasn't thrilled with Brandon wanting her to be his, so long as—

"Is it going to be a problem when I claim *you?*" she asked archly.

He froze, his eyes got all melty, and he stepped closer. "No." His mouth came to her ear, his tongue darting out to taste the lobe. "I'd be honored to be claimed by you."

Her breath caught.

But she was that strong, independent woman.

Which meant that even though his eyes were warm and his tongue made her shiver, she still knew what she wanted.

And that was Brandon.

Oh fuck.

This wasn't considering giving him a chance.

This was him having a direct path to her heart—her realizing he always had.

Pulse pounding, fear and hope, need and longing all twisted up inside her, she stepped back, spun away from him, moving as fast as she could down the hall and into the back yard.

"Fan?" He tried to catch her arm, but she dodged it, kept walking until the cool air was hitting her skin, the moon was bright overhead.

What was she doing?

She should run.

Except . . .

He'd shown up on her porch and shaken her peaceful life, rattling the branches and sending leaves scattering, shattering everything she'd thought was important into irreparable pieces.

"Fan."

She put her hand up, not looking at him. "Please, just . . ."

He paused. She could feel his heat near her, could smell his scent, could hear the quiet rasp of his breath as he held himself back.

She needed to think, to process and—

She also didn't.

Because when all that had been scattered had settled, the broken shards gathered—when she'd read the notebook with all of his mother's memories of them, when he'd surprised her with the basket of gifts, with the certificate to the winery, when he'd cooked for her and offered tonight, when he'd been so gentle with her while taking off her skates, when he'd followed her home, when she remembered the hundreds of other sweet and gentle ways he'd taken care of her before—Fanny knew that irreparable didn't mean forever broken.

She would never be the same.

Neither would he.

There were no guarantees. There never could be. Neither of them could tell the future.

The only thing she *did* know?

That she didn't want to waste any more time.

Maybe the cancer would always be a frightening monster in the back of her mind.

Maybe her heart would always be the teensiest bit broken.

Maybe she would always be worried it might be taken away.

But . . . she could get mowed over by a bus tomorrow. She could get sick and die. She could lose Brandon all over again. And maybe it was the sexy underwear or the heated way Brandon looked at her, inflating her confidence, making her reckless with the urge to jump into things with him with both stilettos, but she also knew the truth.

That she was already *in* with him.

No matter how hard she'd fought in the beginning, she'd been sliding down this slope.

So . . . it was time to let go.

To be with the man she'd never stopped loving, even when she'd been broken into pieces by that love.

Enough time had been lost.

She didn't need to squander any more.

And with that thought, the last remnants of indecision floated away like a balloon flying up into the sky.

"I'm not hungry for food," she murmured.

He straightened, tilted her head back, and stared into her eyes. "What are you hungry for, baby?"

A deep breath, shoving that fear down and locking it up.

Not forever.

Because she didn't want it bubbling back up again. She'd take it out. She'd deal with it. They would build something new, something untarnished by the past.

Something that would mean *everything* going forward.

So when he asked what she was hungry for, Fanny said the only thing she could,

"You."

No hesitation. Not anymore. She was done running and hiding. She was going to grab on to her life, on to this man, and she was going to *live*.

Sixteen

Brandon

His heart swelled . . . along with his cock.

Every cell in his body told him to sweep her up into his arms and fuck her on the next available surface.

But—

He had to make sure.

He'd hurt her before.

He—

"Say something," she whispered, and he'd have to be blind to miss the insecurity creeping into her eyes.

"My doctor says I'm cured."

She rocked back on her heels, her chin jerking up, and that was most certainly the *something* she hadn't wanted him to say, the one thing that could most easily douse the flames of the arousal that had been burning between them from the moment she opened her front door.

"What?" she breathed. "I—"

He'd wanted to tell her, but he shouldn't be telling her in *this* moment. Fuck. Talk about ruining everything, about shoving their past in her face when she'd just finally decided to take a step forward.

"How?" she asked before he could say something, *anything* else.

"I . . . my doctor says that because my scans have been clear for ten years that medically I'm considered cured." He sucked in a breath, released it slowly. "Dr. Lyon says in her professional opinion, she doesn't think it'll come back."

"That's—"

He braced himself.

But she didn't toss words at him. Instead, she threw herself at him. "That's amazing, babe," she said, wrapping her arms tightly around him. "I can't—that's the best news."

Absently, he hugged her back, inhaling her scent and imprinting it on his soul.

"What happened to Dr. Philips?" she asked a moment later.

"He retired and recommended Dr. Lyon. Conveniently, her practice is in San Francisco."

She leaned back, stared at him. "Is that why you came?"

"No." He cupped her cheeks. "I could lie and say it was about my job, my doctor. I might have even told myself that was the reason I accepted Devon's offer. But the truth is that even though I didn't know you were working for the Gold, I knew you were in California, and after I remembered everything, I knew I would take any chance to be closer to you, even if it was just in the same state."

Her lips parted.

She didn't pull away.

"I love you. I wanted to be near you, even when I didn't see how we could have a future. I just knew . . ."

"Magnets," she whispered.

"What?"

"We're a pair of magnets, always drawn together, no matter what comes between us." Half her mouth tipped up. "Cheesy." A shrug. "But—"

"It's the truth," he murmured.

"Yeah."

She fell quiet, and Brandon released her face, gripped her shoulders, and tugged her a little closer, wrapping his arms around her. They stood there holding each other. For once, the past wasn't between them. It was just him and Fanny. She was against him, and he could stand there with her forever.

But then she shifted on her feet.

Slowly, he released her. "Should I cook you dinner now?" he asked lightly, wanting to take her mind off the conversation, off the bomb he'd dropped.

Her mouth tipped up. "Still not hungry for food."

He waited.

"I want you."

His cock twitched, but she shifted again, and he pushed his desire aside. "Am I hurting you?" he asked, dropping his hands and stepping back.

"No." She closed the distance between them. Shifted again, only this time with a wince.

"You winced."

"I did not."

He slanted a look at her, retreated a pace, worry starting to thread its way through his mind. "I saw you. Don't lie to me," he said. "Did I do something—"

"It's my shoes, Brandon. They're sexy, but they hurt like hell."

"Your shoes?" he asked dumbly, his gaze dropping to her feet.

"Yes, honey. They're tall, they're pointy, and they're—*ah!*"

He swept her up into his arms, started for the stairs.

"What are you doing?" she exclaimed, her hands coming to his shoulders and holding on tight.

"Feeding you," he said, bounding upstairs, pushing one door open and peeking inside to find an office. Then another to find a bathroom.

"Feeding—" She shook her head. "Bedroom is last door on the right."

"Thank fuck," he muttered, heading there and bypassing what felt like a hundred doors in front of him to check. It was two, two more to look beyond, but she'd saved him the trouble, so he moved straight to that last room on the right, pushed through the wooden panel, and took approximately one second to scan the space before heading directly to the bed and setting her on it. "Sexy shoes," he said softly, kneeling in front of her and pressing a kiss to her ankle. He tugged off the first heel, rubbed her foot, noticing the red marks visible even through the stocking she wore, and ordered, "You're never wearing these again."

"I am," she said. "Just next time, we'll do a lot less standing up and talking."

He grunted, yanking the other heel off and tossing it over his shoulder. "Fine," he grumbled, knowing that he wouldn't be able to say no to her. He bent and kissed the red marks, chuckling when she squirmed against his fingers slightly tickling the soles of her feet.

"Brandon?"

He was kissing his way up her calf, her knee, her thigh. "Hmm?"

"Will you come up here?"

"Yes." He just had a pit stop to make. He inched the short skirt of her dress up, exposing . . . a narrow strip of lavender elastic, and froze. "Fanny?" he asked after a moment, leaning in to kiss the small half circle of skin on the inside of her thigh.

"Mmm?" she asked, her legs spreading as much as they were able with the tight skirt holding them close.

"Are you wearing a garter belt?" He darted his tongue out, tasted her skin, and bit back a moan.

She smelled of roses and caramel, tasted sweet and floral, and when he allowed his eyes to flick up, to glance beneath her dress, he saw that her panties were soaked, so much so that the pale purple had become nearly translucent.

"Mmm-hmm," she said, her eyes closing.

"Why?"

"Because I like them." Her breath hissed out when he ran his tongue beneath the thin elastic, drawing it up, up, up—

Until—

He stood, yanked Fan to her feet, and took advantage of her surprise to locate the zipper—under her arm—he tugged it down, peeled the fabric away, and—

It was a miracle he even had any blood left in his body.

It felt like it was all in his dick.

Because he'd pulled back that black material, tugged it up and over her head, let it fall down to puddle on the floor, and . .
.

She was the most beautiful thing he had ever seen.

Her breasts were encased in a lace bra that did absolutely nothing to hide her hardened nipples, and when he let his gaze lower over the curve of her stomach to see her hips covered in more lavender, and those black stockings . . .

"Fucking hell," he muttered.

"Off," Fanny ordered, reaching for the lapels of his jacket and shoving it down his arms, leaving him to wrestle with it as she started unbuttoning his shirt. They struggled with the material, and as they did so, he cursed his decision for the suit. He should have put on a T-shirt and jeans. It would have been much easier to take off.

But finally, he managed to sling his jacket across the room, and Fan finished with the shirt buttons while he stepped out of his shoes, and shoved down his pants, yanked off his socks.

Then he was just in his boxer briefs, and she was in her sexy, little outfit, and *then* he got back to doing what he wanted to do before.

He nudged her to sit on the edge of the bed and knelt between her thighs.

And he had *his* dinner.

Her panties were tugged to the side, those elastics unsnapped, and her legs spread wide. He used the flat of his tongue to lick her from bottom to top, once, twice, and when her hands flexed on the mattress, he arrowed in on her clit, sucking it deep as he slipped a finger inside.

It was new, and not.

It was familiar, and not.

His body remembered what to do, remembered what she liked, or *had* liked then, but she'd changed, and so had he. There was relearning to be done, things to discover, things to let go of, but it wasn't difficult, and it didn't take long before he'd homed in on what made her moan and writhe and eventually—when he crooked his finger just right, when he sucked her clit hard—scream.

"Brandon!"

Her fingers clenched his hair, her thighs clamped tight around him.

And then slowly, like a wave creeping up a shore, she relaxed, her shoulders slumping, hands releasing, legs spreading wide.

Desire a heavy beat in his heart, he tossed her back up on the bed, coming on top of her and taking her in his arms. He kissed her long and slow, until her relaxation turned into tension, until that tension turned into need, until that transformed into something more, into something that pushed him over the edge. He scrambled off the bed for his pants, reaching into the pocket and pulling out his wallet. He yanked out a condom, tore the package open with his teeth. A second later, he was rolling it down the hard length of his cock, climbing back on top of Fanny, spreading her thighs, and positioning himself between them. He paused, waiting until she looked at him, wanting to make sure she was ready for this, ready for him, ready for them to take this step.

Every cell in his body was screaming at him, every nerve was on fire, every muscle ached, and his control hung on a razor's edge.

Thrust home. Take them both over the edge. It would be so easy.

But this was Fanny.

This was the woman who held his heart. There was no way

that he would allow himself to take advantage of her in any way, shape, or form.

He loved her.

If she didn't want this, he would stop.

Even if that meant he would be going home with blue balls.

But poised between her legs, his cock one inch from salvation, sweat dripping down his spine, every part of him tense and needy, he prayed she wouldn't turn him away.

"Fanny," he said, his voice a rasp, "look at me."

Her eyes were closed, her head tossed back on the pillow, sweat turning her skin a golden color in the dim lights of the bedroom. "Brandon," she begged, reaching for him, tugging at his shoulders, drawing him down toward her.

He was desperate to push home, desperate to feel her wrapped around him again.

But he wouldn't slide inside that slick heat, not until he saw she was ready.

"Fanny," he demanded again, "*look at me.*"

Her eyes peeled open; those deep brown irises met his. He saw his desperation mirrored in her own gaze, felt the need making her hands shake as she clung to his shoulders.

But he needed the words.

"Do you want this?" he asked, brushing her hair off her face. "Do you want me like this?"

Her nails dug into his skin, a sharp bite of pain that threatened to shatter his control, but he held on. He'd waited a decade for this, he could wait until she was ready.

"Brandon." Her fingers dug in a little harder. "Look at me," she demanded. "*Really* look at me. Have I given you any indication that I don't want this? I'm naked and beneath you. I'm wet. I'm needy."

"Baby," he began.

"I'm still shaking from my orgasm, my legs are spread, my pussy is aching for you. I want you inside me. I want you to fuck me until we both can't see straight. And then"—she cupped his face in her hands—"I want you to do it all over again. I want to remember you were between my legs when I'm skating tomorrow. I want to feel sore and wrung out and thoroughly used, and—"

His control snapped. He thrust home, bottoming out, feeling the liquid heat of her surround him.

She was tight. She was everything he remembered. She was so much more than he had ever hoped.

"And then I want to come home, and I want you to have missed me so much that you fuck me the moment I walk through the door," she said, her eyes blazing, her legs wrapping around him, her hips meeting his as he began to thrust. "I want everything. I want you in every room of my house. I want you in every room of yours. I want to make up for all the things that we missed out on. I want the sex. I want the fucking. I want you to make love to me." She moaned when he thrust a little deeper, arching against him. "And I want the rest of it, too. I want the dinners together. I want to wake up with you wrapped around me. I want to watch bad TV shows together. I want to look up from a class and see you sitting in the bleachers. I want you in my life no matter what the future brings. I just want you, Brandon."

"Fanny," he breathed, so touched that his eyes begin to burn. He blinked back the tears but felt one escape anyway; Fanny reached up and wiped it away.

"I want it all, too," he told her. "We missed out on so much time together, and I don't want to waste any more. I love you, and I will love you for far longer than my body will be on this planet. I will love you like the wind caresses the shoreline, the mountains, the desert, and the sea. Always there, even though sometimes you can't see it. I will love you with every single piece of me, whole, broken, or somewhere in between. I will—"

She sat up, wrapped her arms around him, knocking him back to his knees. "*God*, I love you."

Brandon's heart seized.

"I won't love you like the wind," she said. "You'll see my love for you every single minute of the day. You'll know that I'm here, that I fell for you when I was fourteen and that I've never felt the same way about anyone else." Tears streaked down her cheeks. "I know I'm still broken. I know the pieces are duct-taped together and a bit dinged from life, from our past, from the hurt I held on to for so long." He kissed those salty streaks of moisture away, held her tight. "But they're all yours. They've always been yours, and they always will be."

He was the luckiest fucker on the planet.

"Now," she said, lying back and drawing him down on top of her again, "you're naked and inside me. I'm naked and wetter than I've ever been in my life. Please, *please* fuck me."

His throat burned. He knew he still had tears clinging to his lashes.

But his woman needed him to give her another orgasm, and frankly, he needed one, too.

It had been too fucking long.

So, he began to move, mixing the new and old, the learning and remembering, the knowing and discovering, and he found a rhythm that had her matching his movements, meeting his thrusts. She writhed beneath him, bucking as her fingers clung tight, her nails digging into his shoulders, her hips pressing to his, over and over and *over* again.

And then she fractured, her eyes slamming shut, tossing her head back, her body stilling as her pussy clenched tight around him.

He let the pulses tug him over the edge, stroking into her as his orgasm swelled up and sucked him under.

He came to, somehow on his side, Fanny tucked against him.

They didn't say anything for long moments, didn't speak as their breathing slowed, as the sweat cooled on their bodies, and he pulled the blankets up and over them.

She was so still and quiet, that she could have been asleep.

And yet, he knew she wasn't.

"I love you," she said softly, "just in case you thought it was in the heat of the moment."

Brandon's mouth turned up, and he kissed the top of her head. "Good," he murmured. "Now"—he let his voice raise in volume—"should I cook you dinner?"

Her laughter was the best sound on the planet.

He soaked it in . . . and then he went downstairs and cooked his woman dinner.

SEVENTEEN

FANNY

"Oh, my God," she said. "Now they're *trying* to lose money."

"I know," Charlie said. "Isn't it great?"

She giggled like a loon, as she often did with this man. They'd grabbed drinks and food a couple of times since their dinner and now had a standing friend date on Wednesday nights. Scarlett was jealous and often crashed their time together, but seeing as she couldn't stand the terrible reality show they were currently binge-ing, she'd skipped that night.

The reality show in question followed a bunch of sexy people who liked to bone with no strings attached but couldn't because doing so meant they would lose out on the grand prize at the end.

"I've said it once"—she picked up her wineglass—"and I'll say it again. If I were them, stuck at a luxury resort for several weeks, with all the free booze and drinks I could get, I'd be boning left and right."

Charlie cackled as he clinked his glass to hers. "Damn right, you would," he said, then pointed at the screen. "Oh no, here they go."

She smirked.

Because damn right, they did.

They went. They kissed and cuddled and lost a boatload of money. It was glorious.

Fan and Charlie kept up their commentary through one episode and into the next, during which Brandon came over to her place—with a key she'd given him because . . . not looking back. He took one look at both of them on the couch then the TV and shook his head. Then he picked up both of their glasses, went into the kitchen, and refilled them.

Things had been a little testy between him and Charlie at first —more from Brandon's side than Charlie's, since the latter didn't know about the Hallway Incident. But as she was learning about Charlie, he'd quickly disarmed Brandon, and now the two were casual friends.

She'd take it.

She liked Charlie, and things would have been really awkward if Brandon had gone all He-man protective alpha on her.

But then again, he wouldn't do that.

Because Brandon was Brandon.

He cared about her and what made her happy. Charlie being her reality TV show watching buddy made her happy. Along with the stories he told her while they were out to drinks or dinner, even though those drinks and dinner sometimes took Fan away from Brandon (sometimes Bran tagged along, and sometimes he didn't).

When she'd asked Brandon if he had an issue with her being friends with Charlie—not that she would stop, because it was her freaking life (though she could be friends in a way that made Bran more comfortable, if necessary)—he'd simply asked if Charlie made her happy. She'd nodded. Then he'd smiled, kissed her cheek, and told her to have fun.

Though it should be noted that before she'd left, he'd pulled her close, kissed her within an inch of her life, then murmured in her ear, "No hallways."

The murmur was more order than not.

But anyway.

Now she and Charlie were close, and she got to see more of Scarlett when she wasn't traveling with the team, by benefit of her coming over to hang with Fan and her brother, a la two birds one stone.

Brandon plunked the glasses on the table just as she and Charlie squealed.

"They're not going to have anything left," Charlie exclaimed, picking up the glass and taking a large sip.

"No, they're not." She grinned at him and then sipped before turning to Brandon. "Thank you."

A tug of her hair before he disappeared back into the kitchen.

She was firmly in Reality Show Fog when he returned, a beer in hand, and slid next to her on the couch, his arm coming around her shoulders. He kissed her temple, and she snuggled in to watch, perfectly content in Brandon's arms.

It wasn't until later that she realized she'd fallen asleep.

The show was paused on the TV. She was tucked on the couch, a blanket around her, and when she turned her head, she could see Brandon and Charlie talking in the hall.

"Thanks for being cool with this," Charlie was saying quietly. "She's . . . incredible, but I want you to know that I wouldn't overstep, and neither would she. We just like hanging out, and she's made it clear that we're friends and nothing more."

Brandon nodded. "I know. I trust her." A beat. "Maybe not you, but I trust her."

Charlie smiled wolfishly. "I get it. A woman like that makes a man take notice, but I promise that I'll respect the boundaries she laid out. Friends. Nothing more."

Brandon nodded again, and if she hadn't had so much wine, and hadn't been up so early at clinics that morning, and wasn't so warm and cozy under the blankets on the couch, she would have gotten up and told the both of them what she thought about them discussing her like she wasn't in the room.

Or the next room, anyway.

But she was tired, and a little buzzed, and more than a little snuggly. So she didn't get up and tell them off. Instead, she let her eyes close again, burrowed into the couch, and drifted off.

She was exhausted and slightly drunk and cozy.

She still distantly heard Charlie leave and even more distantly felt Brandon pick her up off the couch and carry her upstairs, tucking her under the covers before slipping in beside her.

"How much money did they lose?" she murmured, burrowing into all of *his* snuggliness.

A beat, his fingers drifting through her hair. "All of it."

She smiled, pressed her lips to his throat, and was tugged completely under.

———

They had gone to the movies. They had stayed in and cooked dinner. Brandon had waited for her after clinics at the rink, and she stayed at his place.

They had spent ten years apart, and yet, over the last month, it felt like no time had passed at all.

And now, she was looking forward to using the gift certificate he had given her, only instead of using it by herself as she'd thought she might when she'd first opened that envelope, he was by her side.

As they walked through the space where she once dreamed her wedding would be held.

The sun was shining, the wind was floating through the vines. Brandon held her hand, and they both had taken on a quiet that was somehow both hopeful and tense, as though they were both expecting the past to come up, dig its claws into them, and drag them both under once again.

But as they flowed through the space, the sun still warm, the wind still gently blowing, Fanny found herself beginning to relax.

The past was just that. Past.

And she was done letting it have a hold on her.

So, she just kept taking steps forward, continued feeling the sun, continued feeling the wind, continued feeling Brandon holding her, and . . . she let go.

"I remember visiting this place," she murmured, holding Brandon's fingers a little tighter. "I remember thinking that we'd be so happy here. I remember thinking this would be the start of us. And in a way, it was."

Brandon turned to face her, his eyes full of old pain and she felt an answering echo in herself.

But that wasn't why she'd brought it up. That wasn't why he'd bought her the certificate for this place. They weren't trying to revisit old pain, to drive their fingers into the open wounds that were still healing. They weren't even trying to slap a Band-Aid on to those lesions, trying to stitch them up or cover them over.

Instead, they were trying to live.

Trying to face those hurts and move on.

"I was so convinced it was our turn to have our happiness," she whispered, "and I was broken when it didn't work out."

His jaw clenched and he dropped her hand, fisting both at his side. "I will never, fucking *ever*, forgive myself for hurting you that way. The first time was bad enough, but the second time, with Angela, with all those months you spent trying to get me to remember—"

"I will never regret fighting for you," she said, taking his hands and unfurling them. "Just like I would never, *ever* begrudge you your happiness, even though it didn't include me. Yes, I was broken. Yes, I had to start over. But I'm not broken today. I'm not living half a life. I have friends and a job. I have a career I love, and . . . I have you, which is the freaking icing on the cake, because I never thought we'd be here again." She smiled. "I never thought I'd be open to it, vulnerable to all I feel, if I'm being honest."

"Fan," he whispered, reaching up and swiping a hand over her cheek, capturing a tear on his thumb. "I don't want to hurt you—"

"I know," she said. "That's what always made it so hard before. You were still so damned nice, even when you didn't feel the same for me. Always polite, even though I was there *all* the time, and you had to want to get rid of the pesky girl who kept making you look at photo albums and listen to songs, hoping it would spark something." She slid a little closer. "But you not wanting to hurt me is also what makes that risk bearable today. I could lose you in an instant. I could die tomorrow and leave you. We have this one life, and I'm done living behind protective walls, just because I might not come out unscathed if I step beyond them."

He slipped his fingers into her hair, trailed them down her throat, playing with the strap of her dress, his rough callouses on the skin of her shoulder making her lips part on a sigh, her body shift even closer.

"What did I ever do to deserve you?" he murmured, bending his head and inhaling deeply, as though he wanted to imprint her scent on to his soul.

"You were you," she said. "And that's enough."

His head came up so quickly that she jumped, but she didn't have a chance to do more than meet his blazing eyes before his fingers had wrapped around her wrist and he was tugging her forward.

"What—"

He scooped her up when she stumbled, pushing through the vines and walking unerringly in the opposite direction from the way they'd come.

"Brandon?" she asked.

He kept walking.

"What are you doing?"

His gaze met hers for a heartbeat, but that short beat of time was enough to have her thighs pressing together, desire a heavy wave of need flowing over her skin, taking the place of the sun, of the wind. "When we came here to scout wedding sights, I did some scouting of my own."

He pushed through a final row of vines, and she gasped at the sight in front of them.

A deep blue pond, grass—what would have been brown just a week ago, having turned green and lush from an unusual rainstorm just a few days before—surrounding its edges. Large, old growth oaks dotted the space, growing very close together near the water, as though they needed to soak in as much as they could—and they probably did, considering how often the area was in and out of droughts.

This place was California's version of a mirage, tall weeds with small, yellow flowers in the distance, the wind just strong enough to keep the bugs away, the pond looking even more blue from the sky reflected above.

Even the birdsong was mellow, just soft enough to create a beautiful background melody.

It was . . . peace.

It was perfect.

This was where she would like to get married. If she were choosing a spot as the woman she was now, not worrying about guest lists and a dance floor and a space for a DJ, *this* would be it.

She and Brandon. The sun shining overhead. Their future on the breeze, in the birdsong, in the warmth of the air.

But while she was reveling in the peace, in the fact that this man had known her so well then, knew her just as well now, Brandon had other ideas.

"I'd planned on stealing you away during the reception," he murmured, striding down the hill. "I'd planned on stashing a basket here"—he set her down gently, holding her while she found her balance, then reached between two of the trees to retrieve a wicker container—"and a blanket here." He reached up, and she saw what she'd missed before, the blue plaid material hanging from the branch. "I'd planned on starting our wedding night under the stars and the moonlight, with promises of bringing them both to you, if you only asked."

Love.

It could be a devastating feeling, could bring someone to their knees, destroy them and yank the foundation of their being out from beneath them.

Or it could be *this*.

Filling her up until she felt like she was floating, until the old cracks were sealed, until she was herself and . . . more.

"So, give it to me," she breathed, stepping toward him. "Give me every part of you, and *more*. Give me the moon and the sun and the stars in the sky and give me *you*."

One second, he was standing there, the blanket in his arms, the basket at his feet.

The next *she* was in his arms, the blanket on the ground, his mouth descending. "It's already yours."

And then he kissed her.

It wasn't the frenzy of their first time, Fanny feeling like she was out of control, like she needed to have him *right* then. Oh yeah, she wanted him. Oh yeah, she was wet and aching. But this was more; this *meant* more. This was the beginning, their future. The sun, the moon, and the stars.

He laid her onto the blanket, his weight following her down.

"I love you so fucking much," he breathed in her ear, the hot words sliding over her skin, dipping down between her thighs. Then he shifted slightly, his front to her side as he dragged his mouth down her throat, along her collarbone, nudging the straps of her dress to the side, trapping her arms at her sides. A moment later, his hand was beneath her, sliding up her back and finding the tag of her zipper. He slid it down.

Naked skin exposed on a warm fall day.

He tugged the material of her dress down slowly, exposing the tops of her breasts. Lower still, catching on the tips of her hardened nipples.

Her lips parted on a breath, and she inhaled sharply, the pleasure arrowing straight for her pussy. She knew she was wet. God, she'd been plenty wet with Brandon over the last month, but in this moment, she didn't think she'd ever been wetter. She could actually feel the moisture of her arousal soaking through her underwear, dripping down her thighs, making her thighs slick as they slid across one another.

Hot breath on her skin, fingers flicking open her bra, parting the material.

Lips circling, descending, closing in, and then he was sucking her nipple deeply into his mouth, his groan rumbling through her flesh, her moan loud and mixing with his.

"Oh, God," she breathed, when he released her, drifting over to her other breast.

More sucking, more pleasure coiling, more damp heat between her legs.

"Bran," she urged, reaching up and grabbing his shoulders, trying to bring him more on top of her. He stayed at her side, his hands sliding up and down her body, his mouth on her breasts, and then inching slowly.

Only inching.

Slow. So *damned* slow.

When all she wanted was him *in* her.

But no matter how hard she pulled, he didn't speed up, didn't shift over her.

Instead, he continued with that inching, tugging her dress down, sweeping it off her legs. Her panties followed suit, and then she was naked beneath a huge oak tree, sprawled on a blanket, with Brandon worshiping her until she was a shaking, desperate heap of a woman.

He inched over her stomach, kissing along the smattering of freckles there, nipped her hips, and finally crawled over her, pressing her legs wide as he dipped his head and got to work.

Slow and steady, so fucking *slow*.

But good. Glorious even. Gentle licks, unhurried strokes. Every single one ratcheting her up, tightening every muscle, her desire a fire through her veins.

And then just as slowly, she came apart at the seams.

The pleasure slid outward, starting at her center, flooding her torso, her arms, her legs. It spread inexorably forward, shooting out her fingertips and toes, crawling up her neck, across her face, and she would be shocked to find that her hair wasn't on fire.

Maybe she might bother to check, if she could lift an arm.

Brandon stayed between her thighs, gentling her with those slow licks, the delicate circles, and when she expected him to get naked and climb on her, to thrust deep and fast and furious, he stayed slow and gentle, and incrementally ramped her arousal again, until her breaths came in rapid pulses, sweat coated her body. She'd lost her capacity for words, could only make pleading sounds.

But then—*finally*—he stripped off his clothes.

She wanted to worship him like he'd paid homage to her body, but she didn't have time or energy to bring voice to that request, before he was rising over her and sliding home anyway.

Unhurried strokes, reverent touches.

Crawling toward the precipice, not rushing, easing up and up and—

She almost didn't want it to come, wanted to stay like this with Brandon forever, and he seemed to feel the same, lingering on the edge for what seemed like an eternity. But eventually, they got too close, and her release almost surprised her, seeming to climb up the cliffside and drag her down, rather than her plummeting over the edge.

Nirvana in her blood.

The man whom she loved surrounding her, extending a hand to escort her back into reality, even as he found his own climax.

Her name was on his tongue, his body was heavy on top of hers.

But only for a moment.

Then he rolled them to their sides, their chests heaving, their limbs heavy and slick with sweat, and he ran his fingers lightly through her hair.

She summoned some sort of inhuman strength to open her mouth. "I—"

Her stomach growled.

Not just growled, but erupted, shattering the peace. Brandon propped himself up on his elbow, his hair a mess, his eyes warm and layered with humor. "Hungry?"

She didn't get a chance to reply before he tugged his T-shirt over her head, reached for the basket, and began plying her with food.

Her favorites, of course.

Because it was Brandon.

Because she knew he'd take care of her.

They sat on that blanket, next to the pond, watching the sun crawl across the sky, eating the food he'd stashed out here, talking about the past, the present, the future, and just . . . being together

It was perfect.

The absolute most perfect day of her life.

———

Later that week, after she'd been fed and pampered all weekend (and one might say, thoroughly fucked), they'd returned to their new reality.

But that reality was pretty damned great.

Because Brandon was in it.

Because she was finally allowing herself to live it.

"Want some?"

She blinked, knowing she had a sappy smile on her face, but it was impossible to stifle. Not when she was so damned happy. He'd come to the arena tonight, and though she was working, doing some in-game evaluations of the players, he'd seemed to make it his job to make sure she'd eaten enough calories to fuel both teams down there on the ice.

Taking care of her.

She scooped up a hand of buttery popcorn and mock glared at him. "Still think I'm too thin?" she asked before shoving it into her mouth.

He nuzzled her throat as he dropped into the seat next to her. "I'm an asshole."

"Yes," she teased. "An asshole who brings me food and scarves, and takes me on weekends away. Who gives me orgasms, *and* hooks me up with a seat in a fancy box so I can work, all while practically waiting on me hand and foot." She scooped up another handful. "Yup. You're a real asshole."

His lips twitched. "Glad we're in agreement." He leaned close and glanced down at her tablet. She had a notebook whose pages were scrawled with her shorthand, all color-coded. "What are you looking for?"

"Hmm?" She'd gotten lost in his eyes, in the stubble on the strong lines of his jaw.

He pointed to a column on the page. "I've been watching you take notes all game"—it was now final intermission between the second and third periods—"so, what are you tracking?"

She glanced from him to the page then back to him. "You really want to know?"

He lifted a brow but didn't deem to answer.

Probably, because it was a stupid question. Okay, it was *definitely* a stupid question. When had he ever given her any indication that he didn't want to know about her? (And no, she wasn't including during the lost memory years.)

"I use this for the video that Dani sends me," she said, nodding toward the tablet, "but most of that is done after the game because she and her assistants are too busy pulling stuff for the other coaches, and occasionally she's reviewing goals—making sure they're good, or deciding if the on-ice coaches should challenge one that was scored on the team."

"And the notebook?"

"I work with most of the guys in the offseason, tuning up where necessary, making sure their conditioning is solid and prepped for game play." Pride shimmied through her. She liked what she'd built, was happy with what she was doing. "That offseason time isn't just with the Gold. Other players from the league come and see me for private lessons. This"—she nodded at the notebook—"is my little black book. I keep track of the things we're working on, add any new bad habits that they might pick up, all in my patented shorthand."

He grinned. "Chicken scratch is more like it."

"Also that," she allowed. "So anyway, it just helps me stay on track, and though I have a program the team had created for me to track progress, I've found that my color-coded notebook works better for my brain."

"Tell me about the columns."

She kept glancing at him as she explained her system and the color coding, trying to gauge if he'd lost interest in what she was telling him. Typically, this was where people lost their fight in staying interested and their eyes glazed over.

But he was engaged and asked questions that told her he was paying attention.

Which made her feel . . .

Well, it had her leaning up and kissing him soundly on the lips. "I love you."

It made her love him even more.

He ran his thumb along her jaw. "So, tonight is just a check-in?"

"Sort of," she said. "You know I usually work with the whole team during the preseason"—he'd seen her at the practice facility —"but I keep track of guys like Kay, for instance. I want to make sure he's not skating in a way that might exacerbate his injury. And more than that, that he's not picking up bad habits throughout the season." She sighed and shook her head. "Though they do always seem to come back to the ice with them after every break. They're like that Whack-a-Mole game. The moment I fix one, there's another, and then when someone is traded or a rookie joins the roster, I have to evaluate them and then—"

She cut herself off.

"Anyway, that's most of it."

"Fan." He lifted a brow. "We doing this again?"

"I—" She sighed. "You're not bored." He shook his head, causing her heart to flutter. "Brandon?"

His fingers found hers, squeezed. "Yeah, baby?"

"Be patient with me," she said. "I've spent a decade locking down the part of me that wanted a romantic relationship with someone."

Another squeeze, but no hesitation when he said, "Always." He leaned close, brushed a kiss over her cheek. "I'll just have to keep reminding you."

"Will that reminding involve your tongue?"

A wicked smile. "Yes."

"Will it involve your cock?"

His chuckle ruffled her hair. "Yes, love."

"I'm okay with that."

They'd both started laughing when a cry rang out behind them. Used to the children of the Gold running around—screaming, tears, and joy all mixed together and sometimes impossible to tease apart—she set down her tablet and notebook and stood.

Becca—the wife of Brandon's boss, Devon—was holding their son, rocking back and forth, while the little boy cried.

"Sorry," she called. "It's this guy's bedtime."

Fanny was moving before she processed it, closing the distance between them and offering, "Want me to take him for a minute?"

Devon had been pulled out for a quick phone call, even though this was only supposed to be a working night for Fanny— or at least, that was how Brandon had sold the time in the box. She'd protested bringing her work to a situation that was supposed to be for fun, but . . . Brandon was convincing.

So, instead of being in the Gold box or bugging Dani in the video suite, she was here.

With Becca, who was looking exhausted and very pregnant and . . . well, she had two arms, didn't she? And she'd held more than her fair share of kiddos since her tenure with the team. The halls and family suite were practically crawling with them.

"Do you mind?" Becca asked. "I was just trying to pack up our stuff, but he hit the wall."

"I wouldn't have asked if I minded," she said, taking a page from Brandon's book—who she felt approach her shoulder, his fingers lightly grazing her nape, his chuckle in her hair.

"Well, then"—Becca passed Jasper over—"thank you."

The little boy was strongly in toddler mode, which meant that trying to hold him when he was tired and wanting to run around was like trying to wrestle a crocodile.

But Fan was older and stronger, and she'd wrestled more than a few kids off the ice in her day.

She took a little walk around the box with Jasper, pointing out all the exciting things, using her teacher voice that distracted kids who were scared or those who wanted anything but what she was asking them to do. By the time they were on their second circuit of the space, Jasper was less crocodile and more . . . angry panda?

Okay, she didn't know.

He wasn't actively crying or trying to launch out of her arms, at least.

"Do you want kids?" Becca asked quietly.

Fan blinked and rotated away from the painting that had the toddler's attention. Jasper caught sight of his mama and immediately wanted her, so Fanny passed him over. "Yes," she said, her throat going a little tight when Jasper cuddled close and held tight to his mommy's neck. "I've always wanted kids. Hopefully, I'll—"

The buzzer rang, signaling the teams coming out, the same time Dev came back into the suite after finishing his call.

Fanny hurried to extend her thanks and say her goodbyes before heading back to her chair and her notebook.

She slipped past Brandon, and his face was drawn, worry written into the lines around his eyes.

"Are you—?" She started to turn back, but that worry was gone, his normal smile in place, as he shook Devon's hand and said his own goodbyes.

She hesitated for a moment, wanting to make sure he was okay, but the whistle blew.

She needed to do her job.

One more look to make sure that he was all right, another to make sure his expression was back to normal.

Then she moved to her chair, telling herself that she'd imagined the look.

And that decision was catastrophic.

———

"Hey, would you mind sharing the picture they took of us at the winery?" she asked as Brandon unbuttoned the rest of his shirt.

He was hopping into the shower after having spent the day at a photo shoot with Kaydon.

That photo shoot had unexpectedly been moved to the beach after a pipe had burst at the first location, and his suit was not conducive to ocean air and sand. So, she'd met him here at his house instead of the restaurant so he could clean up.

She thought he looked good enough to eat, no cleaning necessary.

His hair was windblown, the tops of his cheeks slightly pink, and his lips were a little chapped.

Surfer Brandon . . . in a suit.

Ha.

But that was why he was showering. They had reservations at the fancy restaurant he had originally booked the night after the raffle, and Surfer Brandon wasn't the Brandon he wanted to be for dinner.

Shame for her.

Especially since he'd banned her from getting in the shower *with* him.

"Do you know what kind of favor I had to pull the first time to get this reservation?" he'd said, nudging her back when she drifted close and began unbuttoning his shirt. "Let alone the second?"

"No," she said, coming close again and wrapping her arms around his neck. "I don't care."

He smelled like the ocean and sunlight, and she wanted to eat him up.

Another nudge back. "I'm taking you to dinner."

Fanny pursed her lips as she stared at him. "Or you could just take *me?*"

He'd groaned and dropped his head. "You're killing me, baby." His lips were a hair's breadth away, and he kissed her until she'd become a lump of need and desire, and then had scooped her up into his arms and carried her to the bed.

She'd thought she won.

But he'd merely dropped her on his mattress and backed away, pausing only to toe off his shoes and socks and tug off his tie.

God, why was that so sexy?

Though not as sexy as him parting the fabric of his shirt, revealing smooth tan skin below as she watched, still on the bed. It was like her private strip show, and she had to say that she was kind of into it. Especially when he unbuttoned his slacks and stepped out of them and there was so much tempting skin on display that she almost forgot she'd asked him a question.

"Sure," he said, nodding to the dresser that took up most of the wall by the bathroom. "It's right here. The code is 1-9-2-2."

Aw.

Those were the dates of their birthdays.

He noticed her face, and his own expression softened. "Told you, I remembered."

"Want to come over and *show* me what you remembered?"

Laughter in his eyes. "You're incorrigible."

"And horny."

More laughter, though this time it was bubbling up his throat and filling the air, and God, she loved that sound, loved that she could make him *make* that sound. Then he turned for the bathroom and she heard the lock *clicking* in place.

"You're not going to bring it to me?" she called.

"Nope." A beat. "Because if I do, we won't make it to dinner."

She pouted . . . for just a moment.

Then the shower came on, and she stopped her pouting, getting up and fussing with her dress—not the sexy black one from before, but a longer midnight blue one that hit just above the knee—in front of the mirror in Brandon's bedroom. She'd paired it with a pair of sexy heels that she could actually walk in and wouldn't be cursing if she had to stand in them for a fair amount of time.

And underneath . . . well, if Brandon knew what was beneath the silk, he wouldn't have been in that shower.

It was expensive.

It was skimpy.

It was sexy as hell.

Satisfied the bed toss hadn't messed up her hair or outfit, she headed to the dresser, snagged Brandon's phone, and then typed in 1-9-2-2. She'd text the pic to herself and then she would get it printed. She already had a plan to put it in the empty space by the entryway so that she could see it every time she came home.

It was a *great* picture, reminiscent of that one from nearly two decades before.

Their arms around each other, smiles on their mouths, laughter and love in their eyes, and the employee from the winery had taken it at the absolute perfect moment.

Probably because they'd spent the afternoon making love outside at the secluded pond, and she'd been half-delirious from orgasms. Either that or filled with shock that they'd somehow managed so much outside naked time without getting caught.

She started to pull up the photo as she moved to grab her purse but tripped over the edge of the rug. Stumbling, his cell nearly flying from her hands, her fingers slipped on the screen, and she ended up jabbing the voicemail icon instead.

"Shit," she muttered, straightening herself—and the skirt of her dress—and tapping the screen to exit back to the photos section, but then her eyes caught on the text of the voicemail transcript she'd accidentally started playing.

This is Dr. Lyon. I have the results . . . Please give me a call right away. It's imperative we make some decisions . . .

Her fingers were frozen.

No, every part of her was frozen.

Results. Call. Imperative. Decisions.

Fuck. Was she losing him *already?*

She'd only just gotten him back and—her hands shook as she set the cell back on the dresser—and now—

Her eyes slid closed. She should . . .

Talk to him. Knock on the door, demand he let her in and ask that he explain how he'd gone from cured to results and imperative decisions.

But . . . she couldn't breathe.

Black was intruding on the edges of her vision, and she stumbled again, this time into the dresser. Her hand came in contact with cool wood, and then she wasn't thinking about talking. She was darting out of the bedroom, sprinting down the hall.

She was out the front door.

She was in her car.

She was driving. Far, far away.

EIGHTEEN

BRANDON

He showered in record time, not trusting Fan to stay in the bedroom.

He half expected her to pick the lock and join him. But she hadn't.

And even though he really wanted to take her to the restaurant—she deserved so much, not the least of which was a nice meal at a fancy place, no matter how many favors he had to call in—he could admit that he felt a little disappointed.

Wet, slick Fanny would never be resistible.

Hell, it had nearly killed him to not climb into bed with her and to shower instead.

Sighing, he thrust a hand through his hair—which was as much styling as he did nowadays—and then wrapped his towel around his waist.

Then he unlocked the bathroom door and moved into the bedroom.

His cell was on his dresser, hers was next to it.

But Fan wasn't anywhere in sight.

"Baby?" he called, yanking open a drawer and stepping into

his underwear. He'd expected to have to fend her off when he came out. But maybe she'd decided to give them both a break and go downstairs.

He tugged up a fresh pair of slacks then buttoned on a blue shirt that would match Fanny's gorgeous dress.

Shoes and socks. His phone in his pocket.

"Fan?" he called again. Maybe she'd taken a call.

No, dumbass, her phone was right next to his. He grabbed hers, too, stuck it in his pocket. Maybe she'd gone out back.

But she wasn't there either.

Nor was she on the couch, having fallen asleep.

Not in the kitchen or the other bathroom. Not in his office reading a book. Not . . . anywhere.

He opened the front door almost robotically, and his heart sank when he saw her car wasn't in the driveway.

Unlocking his phone, he went to call her, forgetting again for a moment that she didn't have her cell. It opened onto the message screen. Onto a new voicemail from . . . Dr. Lyon.

A sinking feeling settled into his stomach, tugging him down, *down*.

"Shit," he whispered, hitting play on the message.

This is Dr. Lyon. I have the results of the tests you asked me for. Please, give me a call right away. It's imperative we make some decisions regarding the status of the samples.

"Fuck!" he burst out after the message ended.

Because it didn't take a genius to figure out what Fan had heard, what conclusion she'd come to. Why she had suddenly disappeared.

Fury coursed through him.

He'd thought they were over this. That they were moving forward.

That they were done letting fear or the past take them down again.

And the *first* time he'd gotten a message about his health, the first *fucking* time, she'd run. What the fuck was that? Look, he got it. She'd been fucked over by the circumstances of his health almost more than he had. But this? This was fucking bullshit, and she needed to know it.

He sighed, trying to cool his temper, but it was nearing on impossible.

Why hadn't she just talked to him instead of disappearing?

Didn't she understand how fucked up that was?

But . . . trauma.

It didn't magically go away just because they were together. And the path to healing wasn't a straight one. Shit went down, things got fucked up, but the real mettle was being a person to fix things. He couldn't fix things before, couldn't make the cancer go away or the memories come back. But he sure as shit could fight for Fanny, could explain what the call was about, and stay, no matter how many times she pushed him away.

He closed the door, but only for as long as it took to grab his wallet and keys before heading back outside and getting in his car.

He knew where she would go.

So, he'd follow. He'd fight.

And then he would make her understand, shake some sense into her until she recognized that their lives were connected for-fucking-ever.

No matter where she ran.

And *then* maybe he'd kiss her.

Okay, he would *definitely* kiss her.

Especially if kissing was the most efficient avenue to get that sense into her.

NINETEEN

FANNY

She didn't realize where she was until her knees were frozen. Literally.

Or they felt that way, anyway.

She was kneeling on the ice, just inside the door to the rink, some sense of self-preservation having kicked in so that her high-heeled self hadn't decided to start Bambi-ing on the ice without her skates.

Unprepared.

That wasn't like her.

She usually kept her skates in her trunk.

But she hadn't been planning on skating, not until Monday. She had *planned* an entire weekend of being in Brandon's bed, ordering food, watching movies, having copious amounts of orgasms, and not surfacing until they both had to get back to work.

She didn't know how she'd gotten to the practice facility or how there wasn't anyone on the ice. This evening slot would normally be a prime slot for public skating or a birthday party or someone might rent it. This was why her practice or head-clearing time came late at night or early in the morning, when no one else was around. But maybe she'd get lucky and could disappear and—

Brit skated onto the ice.

Or not. Because this was Brit's extra ice time. She remembered hearing Brit talk about getting Frankie—the goalie coach—and a few of the Gold players together for an hour so she could work on a couple of things.

And sure as hell, Kaydon, Blane, Coop, and Ethan skated out.

Fuck.

Brit started to head for the net, the guys for some pucks, and Fanny tried to slither toward the door, wanting to run far and away . . . but her fucking heels. And the dress. And—

She grabbed the boards, lifted a leg, and—

"Stop right there, Fanny Douglas!"

Brit's voice echoed through the empty rink, and Fanny found herself halting when she should have kept running.

Kept.

Running.

The words finally penetrated the panicked haze. Because, seriously, what the fuck was she doing? She hadn't even talked to Brandon. She hadn't even gotten an explanation. And even if that explanation was that he was sick, then what?

Was she going to run from him?

Was she going to be the woman who loved him and then just fucking left because he was sick?

Of course not.

"I need to get my shit together," she whispered. "We'll find our way back to each other, no matter what happens, no matter how long it takes. But"—her eyes slid closed—"I want this time. I want him for however long I can have him."

Skates crunching on the ice had her eyes opening just in time to see Brit coming over.

"Want to tell me what you're doing?" the goalie asked.

Fanny nibbled at her bottom lip. She liked Brit. A lot. But Brit was tough and amazing—hello, first female to play in the NHL outside of an exhibition game, the first female to earn a starting role, the first female to win a Cup (twice). She was a total BAMF, and there was no way she had ever done what Fanny just did.

Brit looked her problems in the eyes and then kicked them in the balls.

"Fanny?" Kaydon asked, skating up behind Brit; Ethan, Blane, and Coop, only a few moments behind. "Is everything okay? Are you hurt?"

Ethan's eyes sparked with fury. "Did *Brandon* hurt you?"

Blane's jaw clenched.

Coop's face stayed neutral, but she didn't miss the intense look in his brown eyes.

One word from her, and these men would have her back.

Hers.

And that, more than anything, snapped her back into herself. Because one word, and they would support her. *Her.* Because she was family. Because even if things went to hell with Brandon, even if he got sick, she would have *them.*

She wasn't alone anymore.

She didn't need to continue doing everything in her power to remain safe and lonely in her isolation.

"I fucked up," she whispered.

"What?" Brit asked.

"I fucked up," she said, louder, her eyes flying from Brit to Ethan, desperation clawing at her. "Oh my God. I saw the message, and I panicked, and I ran, and I . . . left him, and—shit" —she scrambled for her purse, seeing it on the two steps that led up onto the ice—"where's my phone?"

Brit dropped to the ice, her pads bumping into Fanny's leg.

Helmet tipped up on her head, she took the purse from Fanny's arm and reached into it.

Ethan slipped a hand under her arm. "Here," he said. "Come on and sit down." He helped her off the rink and sat her on the bottom bleacher.

Then Blane was there, taking off his jersey and slinging it over her head. "You're shivering," he said quietly.

Because she'd blown it and needed to call Brandon, and—

"It's not here," Brit said.

Ethan sat next to her, just as Coop returned with a blanket bearing the Gold logo, wrapping it around her shoulders. "What?" she exclaimed, jumping up and dislodging it. "It has to be there. I need to call Brandon and tell him what happened and ask him to—" She broke off, thrust her hands into her hair, tears burning her eyes. "I need to talk to him as soon as possible. I messed up, and—and I need to go. I should go. I—"

"No," Ethan said, gripping her arm when she would have launched herself to her feet.

"You're not going anywhere," Blane said. "Not like this. You need to take a couple of deep breaths and calm down."

"Calm down?" She threw her hands up, yanking out of Ethan's hold, moving for the doors, the blanket falling to the floor. "I can't calm down! I just torpedoed my chance with Brandon, and I promised I would be there and that I wouldn't let the past come back and haunt us." Tears began sliding down her cheeks. "And then the first time I saw something that might not be smooth sailing, I panicked and fucking ran off. Without my phone. Away from the man I love and—"

"Hey." This time it was Kaydon who caught her arm, and he tugged her to face him. "Listen to Blane. Take a deep breath"— she opened her mouth to protest, but he kept talking—"and I'll go get my phone. You can call him from it, okay? Tell him where you are so you can fix this."

Fix this.

Yes, that's what she needed to do. If she could just talk to him, then she could fix this.

"Okay, Fan?" Kaydon asked, his thumb wiping at the tears streaking down her cheeks and probably fucking up the makeup she'd painstakingly applied before she'd ruined everything. "Fan?"

She blinked, forgetting about the makeup, and nodded. "Okay," she whispered. "Thank you."

A nod, and then he was gone. Coop came up next to her, bundling her in the blanket again and leading her back to the bleachers, where he and Blane sandwiched her, their big, warm, bulky bodies comforting as they waited for Kaydon to come back.

"I'm so stupid," she muttered, her head in her hands. "I can't believe I ran."

Brit had knelt in front of her. "We all do stupid shit when we're in love." She dropped a hand on to Fanny's knee, squeezed lightly. "He loves you. It'll be okay."

"I wish I could be like you were with Stefan," she whispered.

Brit's relationship with Stefan had been in the public eye from the moment they started seeing each other, and Brit had never looked back. She'd grabbed on to her happiness and lived her life without fear drawing her down.

"What do you mean?" Brit asked.

"You were so brave. You knew you would be good together and just went for it," she said. "You didn't let anything or anyone get between you."

Brit's brows had lifted, and they were sky-high by the time Fanny finished speaking. She turned slightly to look at Blane.

Fanny turned, too, saw and felt him shrug. "It's not exactly common knowledge," he said.

Brit sat back on her heels. "Stefan and my relationship was a publicity stunt." Fanny's mouth dropped open. "At first," she added, "and then when it became real, I was terrified. Fucking *terrified* that I was going to do something to ruin it between us, that everything might go wrong, and I'd be hurt."

"You were?"

She nodded. "Love is fucking terrifying."

"Here, here," Blane said.

"Ball withering," Coop added.

Brit patted her knee. "But it's also the best thing that you can ever do."

Fanny thought about all the times she'd had with Brandon— the good, the bad, the tear-jerking, and the moments that had made her feel more complete and happier than she ever dreamed was possible. "Yes," she agreed, "it is."

Brit smiled at her, patted her knee again. "It'll be okay, Fan."

Fanny could only hope that was true.

Kay walked back over to them, extending his cell toward her. "Brandon's number is all cued up. Just hit the button, and you can call him."

Fanny started to take it.

"Or," Brit said, her gaze drifting to the left, "you could just talk to him in person."

Fanny's heart thudded once, hard against her ribs.

And then she followed Brit's stare to see Brandon striding through the doors.

"Oh shit," she breathed.

He looked furious.

"Want me to stay?" Brit asked.

"No," she murmured.

"We'll be close by if you need us," Ethan said, pushing up from the bench. He led the others back onto the ice just as Brandon reached her.

She stood, still clutching the blanket, opened her mouth. "I'm so—"

Brandon yanked her against him and kissed her.

She tried to push away from him.

Which was another mistake in the long line of mistakes she'd made that evening.

First, not talking to him. Then running like an idiot and leaving her phone. Now, trying to break a kiss that was clearly trying to show her that while he might be furious, he still liked her enough to kiss her.

"Bran—" she began when he eased up enough for her to form words.

It was formed against his lips, but she didn't even get his full name out before he was kissing her again, his fingers in her hair, his tongue in her mouth, and her body melting against his.

"You're not leaving," he eventually said, pulling back enough so that his words were formed against *her* lips.

"No," she agreed.

He kissed her again, deeper and longer until she could barely see straight. Then he took her hand and started dragging her toward the door, the blanket fluttering behind her like a cape.

She wanted to go home, to allow him to take her away from this.

But she knew that she needed to talk to him first.

"Wait," she began, yanking against his hold.

Brandon spun to face her. "No, Fan. I've been patient. I've understood that it's going to take you some time. I love you, and for a while I considered that it might be better to just let you live your life without the risk of me."

She gasped.

"But I decided that life is too fucking short to not go after what I want, and what I want is you. Forever. For as long as I'm able to have you." He touched her cheek. "And if you get scared again and run off, I'll find you because I know deep down in here" —his hand slid down, covered the spot just above her heart— "that you love me, too, that you want the future and—"

"I do."

She leaned in, pressed a finger to his lips when he tried to go on.

"I love you," she whispered. "I do, and I—I don't want to run. I know it was a mistake, know it was so freaking stupid. I should have just talked to you. I'm so sorry." She cupped his jaw. "But I won't do it again. I promise. I was going back. I was getting ready to call you." She dipped her head toward the rink, where Brit and company were probably soaking in every second so they could report back to the Gossip Train. "Kaydon had just given me his phone so I could call you and tell you how badly I fucked up. I panicked, and I didn't mean to come here and I wasn't thinking clearly, but when I realized what I did, how I reacted, I knew I'd messed up." A tear slipped from her eye. "I don't care if you're sick. I don't care if you forget me. I don't care if you fall in love with someone else." She swallowed hard. "If you don't remember, I'll make you fall in love *with* *me* again. I'm done running. You're worth better than that." She sucked in a breath, released it. "*I'm* worth more than that. I—"

He snagged her hand, kissed her palm. "Fan?"

She blinked, all the words she needed to say still swirling around in her mind, ready to tumble off her tongue. But they all got tangled in her throat, and all she could say was, "Yeah?"

"You'll *make* me love you?"

Her chin came up. "Yes."

"Babe," he murmured, and she couldn't read his face.

More words tumbled out. "I fucked up," she said. "I'm so sorry. I won't leave again. I promise I don't care if you're sick. I'll be there and—"

Soft hands on her face. "I'm not sick."

She blinked. "What? But the phone call—"

"Was from my doctor," he said gently, winding an arm around her waist and drawing her even closer. "She was following up because I asked her about the status of my sperm on ice."

"Uh—" Fanny was stunned into silence. "Um . . . what?"

He bent close, rubbed his nose against hers. "I banked it the first time I got treatment. I was told that I might not be able to have kids after the chemo." He kissed the tip of her nose and straightened to look into her eyes. "I saw you with Jasper, sweetheart. I heard you tell Becca that you want to have babies. I don't know if I can give them to you naturally, but I will try, and if not, we have the samples."

"But the message said it was really important that you make some decisions."

"She needs me to decide if I'm going to pay to relocate the samples out here, or if I'm going to keep them on ice back home."

"That's it?"

He smiled. "That's it."

"And I—" She broke off on a groan, pressing her hands to her face. "Oh, God."

Brandon was gentle when he peeled her fingers back, gentle when he brought her close, gentle as he held her against him. "You were coming back?"

She nodded. "I'm such an idiot."

"You were coming back," he said. "That's all that matters."

Her eyes prickled, and tears threatened to escape again. God, she was so stupid. "I'm so—"

"Fan?"

This time it wasn't Brandon saying her name. She turned to glance at Ethan. He'd come off the ice, or maybe hadn't been shepherded onto it in the first place. Not that Brit was going through her workout. Nope. She, Blane, Kaydon, and Coop were staring through the glass watching them.

Yup.

Gossip Train fodder.

"Yeah?" she whispered to Ethan. His face was soft, his tone even more so.

"You're not an idiot." He tugged her from Brandon's arms, wrapped his own around her, and bent to whisper in her ear, "You're not. Now, I know something of women who run when they're scared."

She leaned back.

He held her close and met her eyes. "*I* know what it's like to be scared and make mistakes. But I know that when you can let that go, you'll have something amazing."

Her lips parted. "You make it sound so simple."

"You've already made the decision to go for it," he said. "That's half the battle."

"I—"

Brit tapped her stick on the glass, and they all whirled to face her. "Go home and make it up to him!" she called. "Makeup sex is the best sex!"

Brandon snorted.

Ethan sighed.

Fanny found herself grinning for the first time since she'd come to the ice, and the guilt twining through her insides all but disappeared when she glanced at Brandon and saw that he was smiling, too. "What do you think, baby?" she asked. "Should we try our hand at makeup sex?"

Ethan snorted this time.

Brandon's smile widened.

Then he took her hand, hauled her away from Ethan, and kissed her senseless.

When she surfaced, Brit and the others were cheering. Brandon nuzzled her throat, nipped at her ear.

And then he took her home.

And Brit was right because makeup sex was the absolute best. It was made even better when paired with her sexy as hell underwear (which convinced Brandon that he didn't really care about the favors he'd had to call in to get the fancy dinner reservations that they'd missed . . . for a second time).

But what made it the best was Brandon holding her close afterward, stroking her hair, and saying, "Babies?"

She smiled and rolled to face him, knowing that while all the fear of losing him hadn't been erased and probably never would be, that she wasn't giving up. Shifting, she rested her hand on his chest, leaned down, and stared into those gorgeous deep brown eyes as she declared, "I can't *wait* to have babies with you."

"Fuck," he hissed.

Fan pulled back slightly, thinking she'd hurt him somehow. "What?"

His hand rested on her hip, tugged her back. "Just that *fuck*, I love you."

"Goof," she teased, leaning close to kiss him, not caring when he pulled her to move fully over him so that she could straddle his hips.

That was right where she wanted to be.

The kiss broke. His mouth got to work, was joined by his fingers.

Pleasure began to coil, her pussy was drenched, need had her wanting to slide down and take him inside—

Wait a minute.

"Why condoms?"

Brandon's forehead was sheened with sweat, his cock was rock hard just millimeters from where she was desperate to have it. His eyes . . . well, his eyes said he didn't give two shits about her question, only that he get inside her and send them both into oblivion.

"What?" he rasped.

"Why have we been using condoms all this time if you can't have kids?"

He blinked. Once. Twice.

Then he flipped them, pressing her back down into the mattress. "I don't know if I'm definitely shooting blanks, baby. Figured it was better to be safe than sorry."

She smiled.

"Any more questions?" he asked against her skin, trailing his mouth down.

She bit her lip. "One."

A sigh, his mouth slowing to lave at her belly button. "Lay it on me."

She ran her fingers through those soft curls. "Will you come inside me?"

This time, his blink made her smile. But not for long because he recovered from his surprise quickly. He slid inside, wiping the smile from her face. She groaned, held on tight, and went along for the fucking glorious ride that Brandon gave her.

Stroking deep and hard, steadily driving them both up and over the edge.

It was glorious.

It was perfect.

And then when he rolled to the side and held her tight, whispering in her ear, "I really hope I'm not shooting blanks because that was fun, and I want to do it again," and they both burst out laughing, it somehow grew even more perfect.

Because Brandon was there.

Because she was finally living her life.

Because they had laughter and love . . . and the potential for him to not be shooting blanks.

P.E.R.F.E.C.T.

Epilogue

BRANDON

They were lying in bed, as had become their habit, talking about nothing, one of Fanny's movies on in the background.

They still hadn't made it to that fancy restaurant.

He couldn't give two shits.

Because he had Fan in his arms.

But it had been six months since that night when everything had threatened to fall apart but instead had all come together, and he figured it was time.

He slipped from the bed, pressing a kiss to Fanny's head when she asked where he was going. He'd just moved into her house that morning, and his boxes were stacked at the edge of the bedroom (and in plenty of other places), but what he needed was in the suitcase he'd stashed in the closet.

Deep down, beneath some other papers. He'd stumbled upon it when he'd cleaned out his filing cabinet.

Another notebook.

Only this time, it was one he'd written in.

One he'd started after his second surgery.

There were entries of being in the hospital and going through physical therapy, cataloging his recovery, jots of the things he remembered.

And drawings. Later, after she'd gone, there had been so many drawings.

All of one thing.

He brought it back to her, along with the folder he'd had put together for just this moment.

"What is it?" she asked, sitting up, the blankets tucked around her chest.

"This," he said, handing it to her.

Fanny froze, then slowly her eyes came back up to his. "What is this?"

"I think you know," he murmured, climbing on the bed and sitting down next to her.

Her gaze dropped, her fingers tracing over one of the pages, over the drawing of a house. Then flipping the page and seeing the same drawing, again and again and again. There were different details each time—outside a wraparound porch, a large back yard with a pond similar to the one they'd made love next to, a swing set, a winding path leading to above ground vegetable planters; and inside a large kitchen with a huge island, the upper cabinet doors made of glass, a laundry room, a huge sectional, a pantry door with frosted glass emblazoned with the word "Pantry."

Stone and warm wood. Granite and tile. Huge rugs and colorful throw cushions.

He'd drawn every angle inside and out.

Over and over again.

"How?" she breathed.

"I don't know."

This was the house that he and Fanny had dreamed about building. The one they'd discussed from the moment they knew they were going to be together forever. They'd discussed the kitchen on the phone when she'd been touring after her silver medal. They'd talked about furniture after he'd aced his finals. They'd planned the pond when he stayed up late to talk, her lying in his in bed after a tough practice. The pantry was during chemo when he couldn't keep anything down. The swing set after he'd finished with his PT.

It was the culmination of late nights and long conversations on the phone, of long, drugging kisses followed by whispering in each other's ears.

It was all of the small moments, the smiles and laughter, the quiet satisfaction after meals shared, the cool kiss of the night's air when they snuggled together in the back of his truck and stared up at the stars in the sky.

"When did you do this?" she whispered.

"After the surgery," he said, as she flipped another page, "and far after you left, all the way up until I remembered."

Her eyes were glassy with tears when she glanced up at him. Then she went back to studying the pages, slowly turning through each one until she reached the end of the notebook. "It's beautiful," she said gently.

It was.

Because it was their dream.

"So," he said, handing her the other thing he'd retrieved, the folder he'd put together, and taking the notebook. "I was kind of hoping that we might be able to live there."

Fanny frowned. "But it doesn't exist."

He opened the folder, showing her the sheaf of papers. Each packet had a listing of lots of land for sale in the area. Any of which could house their dream, could be the place where they built their future. "Pick," he murmured.

"Bran," she whispered, tears slipping free.

"I—*oof!*" He'd started to lean forward to wipe her cheeks, but suddenly found himself sprawled back on the mattress, her arms around him.

"You wonderful, wonderful man."

Then she kissed him until he forgot about the papers, about

the dream of the future, about everything except for the dream of now.

Of this woman, who'd found the courage to love him.

Of this time together, never promised, always precious.

Of this chance to build something new and never look back.

Only later—*much* later—did they go through the papers and narrow it down to two that they would visit in person.

Then he topped off Fanny's glass of wine, stole a handful of her buttery popcorn, and held her close as they watched a movie that was not full of blood and gore.

But instead, it was filled with love and a happy ending.

And Brandon thought that was pretty damned perfect.

P.E.R.F.E.C.T.

SCARLETT

Fanny all but sailed across the ice, pretty and graceful, and on a love-hazed cloud.

Scar's heart squeezed tight.

It would have been nice if she'd fallen for Charlie, but it was pretty damned great that she'd fallen for Brandon.

Who was working at a table in the corner of the rink, his laptop open, his earbuds in, papers spread out on the chair next to him. Even though he had a cushy corner office at Prestige Media Group, he preferred to bundle up and work where he could see the woman he loved.

A little girl was crying on the ice, but before Scar could make her somewhat shaky way over to her—they couldn't all be graceful silver medalist skaters—Fanny knelt and comforted the little girl, and in just a few seconds, they were both on their feet and back to class.

And Brandon was staring at his woman with warm eyes.

God.

She wanted that.

No. No, she didn't. She wanted to keep working. As assistant publicist for the Gold, her job was to manage the team's social media and do her best to keep the public loving them.

It wasn't hard.

The guys were great.

As great as Brandon was.

"Mrs. Scar."

She blinked, forcing her eyes away from Brandon and his obvious affection for Fanny, and looking down at the tiny boy at her knees. "Hey, Dominic. Everything okay?"

His bottom lip wobbled.

Oh shit.

"Hey, buddy," she said, clumsily getting to her knees. "Talk to me."

That lip kept wobbling and was now joined by tears.

Fuck.

"Candace said that I'm bad at skating."

All the kids were bad at skating. That's why she—equally as bad, or perhaps maybe marginally better, depending on who was judging—was helping out with class. She wasn't good enough at skating to help any other time.

Front and back.

Slow turns.

Doing her best to not eat shit.

And mostly she succeeded.

Unfortunately, she couldn't tell him they were all terrible.

"You're doing really good, buddy," she said. "You're just learning, and I know you'll be good in no time."

The tears were still there, but they were slowing. "Really?" he said, snot trailing under his nose.

"Really," she said, shuddering. She started to pull a packet of tissues out of her pocket, kept there for exactly this reason, but before she could get one out, someone else skated over.

Someone tall and handsome, who had her in a constant battle to keep her panties up and around her hips.

They just wanted to drop right off anytime Kaydon was around.

He had arms that made her drool, a strong jaw with a hint of stubble she wanted trailing over her skin, and lips that would pillow perfectly against hers.

If only they didn't work together.

She liked this job.

She *loved* this job.

Which meant she wanted to keep it.

And while the Gold were a treasure trove of couples working together and living out their happy endings, Scarlett didn't have that track record.

When she was in a relationship, things never went well.

And that unwell transitioned into her life, her job, her happiness.

She had terrible taste in men, and when those relationships ended, her shit got dive-bombed. She lost her job. She got kicked out of her apartments. She was dogged by debt collectors, or psycho ex-girlfriends she hadn't know existed (or were wives, in one case—and not the ex-variety—and the reason the man she'd been dating had become *her* ex), or mothers who were pissed that the wedding they'd been planning without Scar's permission (or their son's, for that matter) was off.

So, suffice to say, she was on a break from men.

It was work and friends and rebuilding her life.

No. Men.

But one look at Kaydon when he'd joined the team made her want to reconsider her hiatus. But it was more than his glorious jaw and yummy stumble. He was nice and talented and was just a really decent guy.

Case in point?

Now.

Kaydon bent next to them, scooped up Dominic. He said

something that made Dom laugh, and he didn't seem to care when Dom rubbed his snotty nose against Kay's shoulder.

His big hand came to the back of Dom's helmet, and then he took off with the little boy in his arms, zigging and zagging through the cones, avoiding the other kids effortlessly.

Dom laughed and held on and by the time they circled back, both man and boy had huge smiles on their faces.

A moment later, Dom's skates were on the ice, Kay holding him steady as he spoke quietly.

Scarlett couldn't make out the words, only could see Dom nod intently before he threw his arms around Kaydon's neck. And, oh sweet baby Jesus, her ovaries, because Kaydon didn't hesitate, just hugged him back and patted him lightly on the helmet before lightly pushing him forward so he could rejoin the other kids. Scar could barely resist the urge to clamp her hands to her heart and sigh, the longing to know him better was so intense.

Used to shoving that longing down—she'd done it for nearly an entire season—she pushed to her feet and continued to patrol the ice, making sure everyone was happy and tear-free and staying far, far away from Kaydon, lest he see that longing.

Eventually—thank God, for her ovaries—Fanny blew the whistle, and the classes were over.

Scar's feet ached, but she started cleaning up the ice, so Fan didn't have to, trying deliberately to *not* notice that Kaydon was picking up cones much more rapidly than she was.

And moving closer to her and her bumbling self.

"I can get this, you know?" he rumbled, skating past her, a pile of cones in his arms.

Much bigger than the pile she'd managed to collect.

"I know," she said.

Not that he could hear her.

He was already on the other side of her ice.

The rink had cleared out. The kids in the lobby, Brandon and Fanny in deep discussion over something at his makeshift work-station. Scar lumbered to the door to the ice, her cones the worst sort of Jenga tower, and managed to just barely climb up the step as Kaydon returned from stashing the supplies around the corner.

"Let me," he began.

She walked right by him.

"Okay," he muttered.

She ignored him. It was much better for her sanity.

But apparently today, he was done with her ignoring him. "What's your problem?" he asked, following her into the narrow hallway.

"I don't know what you're talking about," she said, gracelessly bending so she could place the cones on the stack.

She mostly succeeded.

Mostly because a few tumbled off and scattered on the ground. Stifling a curse, she knelt and started picking them up.

So did Kaydon.

Fucking hell. She was trying to be good.

"Scarlett."

Cones. *Cones!*

She set one on the stack, but because she wasn't paying attention, that setting resulting in knocking over, and the cones went everywhere.

Shit.

She reached for them, hands flailing, trying to shift around without slicing hers or Kaydon's—since he was too damned nice and still helping her—fingers off.

"*Scarlett.*"

A warning this time.

Glancing down, she realized exactly where she was reaching. His crotch. Well, for the cone that was less than an inch from his crotch.

She froze, but before she could pull back, his fingers encircled her wrist.

Warm and a little rough.

Her lips parted on an exhale, and she shivered.

"Scarlett," he said again, and this time his voice was like his fingers, warm and a little rough.

She wobbled. He shifted a little closer, smoothing a lock of her hair off her cheek. "Why don't you like me, Scar?"

Still processing all that warm and rough *and* him smoothing back her hair, it took her a second to process his question. But the moment she did, she unstuck, laughter bubbling up her throat and filling the air.

He let her laugh for a minute before his hand—the one not tracing light and lovely circles on her wrist—reached up and cupped her cheek. "I don't love being on the butt end of a joke, baby."

That stoppered up her guffawing.

His thumb moved, swiped at the skin beneath her eyes, and she realized that she'd been laughing so hard, she had tears on her cheeks.

"You're not a joke, Kaydon."

He was so far away from that it wasn't even funny. *She* was the joke. She was the one who was trying to be good.

She was the one who was going to fail.

Again.

Because she leaned forward, whispered before he could reply, "It's not that I don't like you, Kay. It's that you are the sexiest man I've ever seen."

And then she kissed him.

———

Thank you for reading! I hope you loved meeting Brandon and Fanny! The next book in the Gold Hockey series is CYCLED.
No matter how hard Scarlett tried to be good—
She always ended up being bad.

READ CYCLED HERE NOW>

And if you enjoyed CRASHED, you'll love the sexy, sweet, and close-knit Breakers Hockey crew. <u>The first book in the series, BROKEN, is now live!</u>

The more she falls for Stefan, the more she risks her career... Don't miss the first Gold Hockey book. The over 400 five-star-reviewed BLOCKED is FREE!

"Off-the-charts hot, smexy scenes with one of the best book boyfriends I have come across!" —Amazon reviewer

DOWNLOAD BLOCKED FOR FREE >

I so appreciate your help in spreading the word about my books, including sharing with friends! Please leave a review on your favorite book site!
You can also join my Facebook group, the Fabinators, for exclusive giveaways and sneak peeks of future books.

SIGN UP FOR ELISE FABER'S NEWSLETTER HERE: https://www.elisefaber.com/newsletter

---

Want a free bonus story? Hate missing Elise's new releases? Love contests, exclusive excerpts and giveaways?
Then signup for Elise's newsletter here!
https://www.elisefaber.com/newsletter

And join Elise's fan group, the Fabinators https://www.facebook.com/groups/fabinators for insider information, sneak peaks at new releases, and fun freebies! Hope to see you there!

Gold Hockey Series

Gold Hockey

Did you miss any of the Gold Hockey books?
Find information about the full series here.
Or keep reading for a sneak peek into each of the books below!

Blocked
Gold Hockey Book #1
Get your copy at https://www.elisefaber.com/blocked

Brit

The first question Brit always got when people found out she played ice hockey was *"Do you have all of your teeth?"* The second was *"Do you, you know, look at the guys in the locker room?"*

The first she could deal with easily—flash a smile of her full set of chompers, no gaps in sight. The second was more problematic. Especially since it was typically accompanied by a smug smile or a coy wink.

Of course she looked. *Everybody* looked once. Everyone snuck a glance, made a judgment that was quickly filed away and shoved deep down into the recesses of their mind.

And she meant *way* down.

Because, dammit, she was there to play hockey, not assess her teammates' six packs. If she wanted to get her man candy fix, she could just go on social media. There were shirtless guys for days filling her feed.

But that wasn't the answer the media wanted.

Who cared about locker room dynamics? Who gave a damn whether or not she, as a typical heterosexual woman, found her fellow players attractive?

Yet for some inane reason, it *did* matter to people.

Brit wasn't stupid. The press wanted a story. A scandal. They were desperate for her to fall for one of her teammates—or better yet the captain from their rival team—and have an affair that was worthy of a romantic comedy.

She'd just gotten very good at keeping her love life—as nonexistent as it was—to herself, gotten very good at not reacting in any perceptible way to the insinuations.

So when the reporter asked her the same set of questions for the thousandth time in her twenty-six years, she grinned—showing off those teeth—and commented with a sweetly innocent "Could've sworn you were going to ask me about the coed showers." She waited for the room-at-large to laugh then said, "Next question, please."

–Get your copy at https://www.elisefaber.com/blocked

Backhand
Gold Hockey Book #2
Get your copy at https://www.elisefaber.com/backhand

SARA

"Sorry I messed up your sketch," he rumbled.

She nibbled on the side of her mouth, biting back a smile. "Sorry I stole your hand for so long."

He shrugged. "My mom's an artist. I get it."

Well, there went her battle with the smile. Her lips twitched and her teeth came out of hiding. If there was one thing that Sara had, it was her smile. It had been her trademark in her competition days.

Which were long over.

Her mouth flattened out, the grin slipping away. Time to go, time to forget, to move on, to rebuild. "Thanks," she said and extended a hand.

Then winced and dropped it when her ribs cried out in protest.

"You okay?" he asked, head tilting, eyes studying her.

"Fine." And out popped her new smile. The fake one. Careful of her aching side, she shrugged into her backpack. "I've got to go." She turned, ponytail flapping through the hair to land on her opposite shoulder.

"That—" He touched her arm. "Wait. I *know* I know you."

She froze. That was the second time he'd said that, and now they were getting into dangerous territory. Recognition meant . . . no. She couldn't.

There had been a time when *everyone* had known her. Her face on Wheaties boxes, her smile promoting toothpaste and credit cards alike.

That wasn't her life any longer.

"Thanks again. Bye." She started to hurry away.

"Wait." A hand dropped on to her shoulder, thwarting her escape, and she hissed in pain.

"Sorry," he said, but he didn't release her. Instead, he shifted his grip from her aching shoulder down to her elbow and when she didn't protest, he exerted gentle pressure until Sara was facing him again. "It's just that know I *know* you."

No. This wasn't happening.

"You're Sara Jetty."

Her body went tense.

Oh God. This was *so* happening.

"It's me." He touched his chest like she didn't know he was talking about himself, and even as she was finally recognizing the color of his eyes, the familiar curve of his lips and line of his jaw, he said the worst thing ever, "Mike Stewart."

Oh *shit*.

—Get your copy at https://www.elisefaber.com/backhand

Boarding
Gold Hockey Book #3
Get your copy at https://www.elisefaber.com/boarding

MANDY

Hockey players had the *best* asses.

No pancake bottoms, these men—and *women*—could fill out a pair of jeans. She wanted to squeeze it, to nibble it, bounce a dime—

Mandy dropped her chin to her chest, losing sight of the Sorting Hat cupcakes she'd been pondering.

Blane with his yummy ass had a unique way of distracting her.

No, it wasn't even distraction, per se. He had *always* been able to get under her skin.

And that was very, very bad for her.

"Ugh," she said, tossing her phone onto her desk and standing, knowing that she wouldn't be able to sit still now.

Nope, she needed about forty laps in the pool and a good hard fu—

Run, her mind blurted, almost yelling at the mental voice of her inner devil. *A good hard run.*

Unfortunately, the cajoling tone wasn't completely drowned out. *Some sexy horizontal time with Blane would be more fun—*

But the rest of the enticing words were lost as the roar of the crowd suddenly penetrated through the layers of concrete. Her stomach twisted. Mandy could tell, even before her eyes made it to the television, that it wasn't in celebration of a goal or a good hit either.

This was fury, a collective of outrage.

She was on her feet the moment she saw the prone form lying so still face down on the ice.

Her gut twisted when she spotted the curving line of a numeral two on the back of the player's jersey.

"Not him," she said and the words were familiar, a sentiment she had whispered, had *prayed* a thousand times before. She needed the camera angle to shift, for her to be able to see more clearly *who* was hurt. "Not him."

Then Dr. Carter was on the ice and the player moved slightly, rolling away from the camera, giving a full shot of his back and the matching twos adorning his jersey.

Fuck. Not him. Not Blane.

And that was when she saw the pool of blood.

—Get your copy at https://www.elisefaber.com/boarding

Benched
Gold Hockey Book #4
Get your copy at https://www.elisefaber.com/benched

MAX

He started up the car, listening and chiming in at the right places as Brayden talked all things video game.

But his mind was unfortunately stuck on the fact that women were not to be trusted.

He snorted. Brit—the Gold's goalie and the first female in the NHL—and Mandy—the team's head trainer—would smack him around for that sentiment, so he silently amended it to: *most* women were not to be trusted.

There. Better, see?

Somehow, he didn't think they'd see.

He parked in the school's lot, walked Brayden in, and received the appropriate amount of scorn from the secretary for being thirty minutes late to school, then bent to hug Brayden.

"I'll pick you up today," he said.

Brayden smiled and hugged him tightly. Then he whispered something in his ear that hit Max harder than a two-by-four to the temple.

"If you got me a new mom, we wouldn't be late for school."

"Wh-what?" Max stammered.

"Please, Dad? Can you?"

And with that mind fuck of an ask, Brayden gave him one more squeeze and pushed through the door to the playground, calling, "Love you!" over his shoulder.

Then he was gone, and Max was standing in the office of his son's school struggling to comprehend if he had actually just heard what he'd heard.

A new mom?

Fuck his life.

—Get your copy at https://www.elisefaber.com/benched

Breakaway

Gold Hockey Book #5

Get your copy at https://www.elisefaber.com/breakaway

BLUE

"Thanks for the ride."

"Try not to go out and get a fresh bimbo to ride tonight. I hear STIs on are the rise in the city."

Blue sighed, turned back to face her. "Really?"

She shrugged, smirk teasing the edges of her mouth, drawing his focus to the lushness of her lips. "Just watching out for Max's teammate."

He rolled his eyes. "Not hardly."

"Okay, how about I'm trying to prevent you from spreading STIs to the female populace."

"I'm clean, and I'm smart," he told her. "Condoms all the way."

"Ew."

Except there was something about the way she said it that made Blue stiffen and take notice. Because . . . he stared into her eyes, watched as the pale blue darkened to royal, saw her lips part, and her suck in a breath.

Holy shit.

"You're attracted to me."

Her jaw dropped. "No fucking way," she said, too quickly, pink dancing on the edges of her cheekbones. "You're delusional."

Blue got close.

Real close.

Anna licked her lips.

And fuck it all, he kissed that luscious mouth.

—Breakaway, https://www.elisefaber.com/breakaway

Breakout
Gold Hockey Book #6
Get your copy at https://www.elisefaber.com/breakout

PR–REBECCA

A fucking perfect hockey fairy tale.

Shaking her head, because she knew firsthand that fairy tales didn't exist outside of rom-coms and occasionally between alpha sports heroes and their chosen mates, Rebecca slipped through the corridor and stepped onto the Gold's bench.

Lots of dudes in suits—of both the boardroom *and* the hockey variety—were hugging.

On the ice. Near the goals. On the bench.

It was a proverbial hug-fest.

And she was the cynical bitch who couldn't enjoy the fact

that the team she was with had just won the biggest hockey prize of them all.

"I knew you'd be like this."

Rebecca turned her focus from Brit, who was skating with the huge silver cup, to the man—no, to the *boy* because no matter how pretty and yummy he was, Kevin was still a decade younger than her—leaning oh so casually against the boards.

"Nice goal," she told him.

A shrug. "Blue made a nice pass."

And dammit, the fact that he wasn't an arrogant son of a bitch made her like him more.

She nodded at the cup. "You should go have your turn."

"I'll get mine," he said with another shrug.

She frowned, honestly confused. "You don't want—"

Suddenly he was in front of her on the bench, towering over her even though she was wearing her four-inch power heels. "You know what I want?"

Rebecca couldn't speak. Her breath had whooshed out of her in the presence of all that sweaty, hockey god-ness. Fuck he was pretty and gorgeous and . . . so fucking masculine that her thighs actually clenched together.

She wanted to climb him like a stripper pole.

"Do you?" he asked again when her words wouldn't come. "Want to know what I want?"

She nodded.

He bent, lips to her ear. "You, babe," he whispered. "I. Want. You."

Then he straightened and jumped back onto the ice, leaving her gaping after him like she had less than two brain cells in her skull.

The worst part?

She wanted him, too.

Had wanted him since the moment she'd laid eyes on the sexy as sin hockey god.

"Trouble," she murmured. "I'm in *so* much fucking trouble."

—Breakout, https://www.elisefaber.com/breakout

Checked
Gold Hockey Book #7
Get your copy at https://www.elisefaber.com/checked

"Rebecca."

She kept walking.

She might work with Gabe, but she sure as heck wasn't on speaking terms with him. He'd dismissed her work, ignored her contribution to the team. He'd made her feel small and unimportant and—

She kept walking.

"*Rebecca.*"

Not happening. Her car was in sight, thank fuck. She beeped the locks, reached for the handle.

He caught her arm.

"Baby—"

"I am *not* your baby, and you don't get to touch me." She ripped herself free, started muttering as she reached for the handle of her car again. "You don't even like me."

He stepped close, real close. Not touching her, not pushing the boundary she'd set, and yet he still got really freaking close. Her breath caught, her chin lifted, her pulse picked up. "That. Is. Where. You're. Wrong."

She froze.

"What?"

His mouth dropped to her ear, still not touching, but near enough that she could feel his hot breath.

"I like you, Rebecca. Too fucking much."

Then he turned and strode away.

—Checked, https://www.elisefaber.com/checked

Coasting
Gold Hockey Book #8
Get your copy at https://www.elisefaber.com/coasting

Coop

Without thinking, he caught her arm.

"You're not okay."

She shuddered to a stop when he touched her, not fighting the grip, chin dropping to her chest. "No," she said, "you're right. I'm not okay."

"Who was on the phone?" he asked gently.

Her jaw went tight. "My ex."

Fury blazed through him. "Did he hurt you?" he growled.

A shake of her head. "Not like you're thinking." She sucked in a breath. "He broke my heart."

Coop's own heart gave a twinge. "I'm sorry, Calle. That's—"

"Fucking stupid." Another tear joined the first, dripping down the pale skin of her cheek.

"It's not stupid to have loved someone," he said gently.

Her eyes went fierce. "It's incredibly stupid when the person who supposedly loves you right back doesn't give a damn that you're pregnant."

His jaw fell open. He knew it did.

But Calle? Even, gentle *Calle* had gotten knocked up and—

"Yup," she said, brushing by him. "See? Really *fucking* stupid."

And without another word, she disappeared into the rink.

—Coasting, https://www.elisefaber.com/coasting

Centered
Gold Hockey Book #9
Get your copy at https://www.elisefaber.com/centered

"Watch out!"

The warning came a second too late.

He'd already stepped off the curb, already put himself in range of the car that was blowing through the red light, tearing through the intersection, not giving a shit that there were pedestrians walking—

Well, of all the ways to go, at least this would be quick.

But just as the car came within an inch of him, Liam found himself jerked back onto the curb, his one-hundred-and-eighty-pound frame becoming unwieldy and clumsy.

Kind of like on the ice over the last few years.

That was his last thought before he found himself sprawled, ass first, on the San Franciscan sidewalk.

Gross.

"What. The. *Fuck?*" a female voice snapped.

The same female voice that had warned him.

"Do you have a fucking death wish?" she yelled, causing his eyes to snap open, making him look up at an angel . . . a foot tapping, arms crossed, seriously pissed, and seemingly way too small to have been able to haul his ass back onto the curb female.

Liam thought he just might have that death wish.

Especially if it meant he got to be rescued by a woman who looked like an angel. He opened his mouth to reply.

But apparently didn't work fast enough.

Because the woman, the beautiful, curvy female, made a disgusted noise and strode away from him.

He watched her go, watched that gorgeous ass stride down the sidewalk, and stop outside a storefront.

And suddenly, he thought that, hockey or not, he might just want to stay in San Francisco after all.

—Centered, https://www.elisefaber.com/centered

Charging
Gold Hockey Book #10

Get your copy at https://www.elisefaber.com/charging

"Your feet hurt."

Her brows drew together. "What?"

Logan nodded at her feet, clad in a lovely pair of heels that, while beautiful, were also the equivalent of bear traps—and if that wasn't the perfect metaphor for the man in front of her, she didn't know what was.

"Those heels hurt you." His head tilted to the side. "Why do you wear them?"

She scoffed. "None of your fucking business, Walker."

A smile—slow and hot and sliding like silk over her breasts, her stomach, between her legs. "I knew you'd say that."

"I—"

He held up a box she hadn't noticed, pushed it into her hands when she stepped back. "Open it," he said, voice dropping and joining that silk of his smile to dip between her legs. "If you think you can handle it."

And then he was gone, the door closing behind him, leaving her with a heavy ass bag packed with who knew what, aching feet, and a box in her hands.

A box given on a challenge.

A box he knew she'd open.

Because Charlotte Harris didn't give in or back down. She liked that even less than she liked losing.

So, she opened the lid.

And instantly knew she was in trouble.

—Charging, https://www.elisefaber.com/charging

Caged
Gold Hockey Book #11
Get your copy at https://www.elisefaber.com/caged

"Are you seeing anyone?"

Slowly, she spun back, eyes wide.

"That was my question," he said, when she stared at him in shock. "Dani?" he asked, when she just continued staring at him mutely. "Did I break you?"

A slow shake of her head.

He stepped a little closer, just near enough that she could feel the heat from his body. "No to the breaking you part, or no to the seeing anyone piece?" he murmured.

"The seeing anyone thing," she somehow managed to whisper, despite the fact that the question from a man like him to a woman like her was absolutely one hundred percent unfathomable.

Circling back to sad and single and—

He smiled.

And she actually felt her brain cells collide and fizzle into smoke. That smile was dangerous, could without a doubt, turn her stupid. *Really* stupid.

"Good," he murmured.

Swallowing hard, she nodded, cheeks on fire, and turned away again. "Right, I'll just—"

"Will you go out with me?"

Her fingers went limp. The tablets hit the ground.

This time, the *crunch* sounded much more ominous.

Or maybe that was just her heart.

—Caged, https://www.elisefaber.com/caged

Also by Elise Faber

Checked

Coasting

Centered

Charging

Caged

Crashed

A Gold Christmas

Cycled

Caught

Cap

Breakers Hockey *(all stand alone)*

Broken

Boldly

Breathless

Ballsy

Bewitched

Love, Action, Camera *(all stand alone)*

Dotted Line

Action Shot

Close-Up

End Scene

Meet Cute

Love After Midnight **(all stand alone)**

Rum And Notes

Virgin Daiquiri

On The Rocks

Sex On The Seats

Life Sucks Series (all stand alone)

Train Wreck

Hot Mess

Dumpster Fire

Clusterf*@k

FUBAR (March 29,2022)

Roosevelt Ranch Series (all stand alone, series complete)

Disaster at Roosevelt Ranch

Heartbreak at Roosevelt Ranch

Collision at Roosevelt Ranch

Regret at Roosevelt Ranch

Desire at Roosevelt Ranch

Phoenix Series (read in order)

Phoenix Rising

Dark Phoenix

Phoenix Freed

Phoenix: LexTal Chronicles (rereleasing soon, stand alone, Phoenix world)

From Ashes

In Flames

To Smoke

KTS Series

Riding The Edge

Crossing The Line

Leveling The Field

Scorching The Earth

Cocky Heroes World

Tattooed Troublemaker

ABOUT THE AUTHOR

USA Today bestselling author, Elise Faber, loves chocolate, Star Wars, Harry Potter, and hockey (the order depending on the day and how well her team -- the Sharks! -- are playing). She and her husband also play as much hockey as they can squeeze into their schedules, so much so that their typical date night is spent on the ice. Elise changes her hair color more often than some people change their socks, loves sparkly things, and is the mom to two exuberant boys. She lives in Northern California. Connect with her in her Facebook group, the Fabinators or find more information about her books at www.elisefaber.com.

facebook.com/elisefaberauthor

amazon.com/author/elisefaber

bookbub.com/profile/elise-faber

instagram.com/elisefaber

goodreads.com/elisefaber

pinterest.com/elisefaberwrite

www.ingramcontent.com/pod-product-compliance
Lightning Source LLC
Chambersburg PA
CBHW071105100726
47908CB00008B/2271